THE SUDDEN GUNS

Giff Cheshire

Chivers Press   • G.K. Hall & Co.
Bath, England   Thorndike, Maine USA

This Large Print edition is published by Chivers Press, England, and by G.K. Hall & Co., USA.

Published in 2000 in the U.K. by arrangement with the author c/o Golden West Literary Agency.

Published in 2000 in the U.S. by arrangement with Golden West Literary Agency.

U.K. Hardcover   ISBN 0-7540-4216-2   (Chivers Large Print)
U.K. Softcover   ISBN 0-7540-4217-0   (Camden Large Print)
U.S. Softcover   ISBN 0-7838-9092-3   (Nightingale Series Edition)

The text of this Large Print edition is unabridged.
Other aspects of the book may vary from the original edition.

Set in 16 pt. New Times Roman.

Printed in Great Britain on acid-free paper.

British Library Cataloguing in Publication Data available

Library of Congress Cataloging-in-Publication Data

Cheshire, Gifford Paul, 1905–
  The sudden guns / by Giff Cheshire.
  p. cm.
  ISBN 0-7838-9092-3 (lg. print : sc : alk. paper)
  1. Large type books. I. Title.
PS3553.H38 S83 2000
813'.54—dc21   00–031958

THE SUDDEN GUNS

CHAPTER ONE

The girl danced by the pond, pirouetting and swaying. She stopped for a moment to lean forward and regard her reflection in the placid water. It appeared to satisfy her, for she smiled softly, lost in some far thought.

Pick sat motionless in the saddle, silently watching and speculating about her. Her wet dark hair showed she had been in the water, but she had dressed again. Her calico skirt hung lankly until she whirled once more, when it disked out like a wheel. Her bare legs were long and shapely and nearly as brown as her face and bare slender arms. She stopped, made a little dip with her body, and froze abruptly as she stared up at him and Pecos.

With a bound she swept up a rifle that had been hidden from his sight. There was a surprising change in her face, no longer appealing but turned hard and hostile. A swift motion brought up the rifle and leveled it from her slim thigh. The sights were lined on him, maybe because he was the taller of the two riders she had caught spying on her secret ritual and the only one who was grinning.

'Now, we've only been here a minute,' Pick said placatingly. 'Take it kind of easy.'

Her voice cracked back like the popping of a whip. 'If you've got business, spit it out. If not, get riding.'

'He's right,' Pecos Benton said. 'We just got here. Honest Injun.'

'I said talk or get.' She swung the rifle slightly to cover both of them.

Beyond her the broken Sapphires pitched across a flaming Nevada sky. On the stony bajada in the middle ground stretched the patch of trees that gave these springs the name of Joshua, or Josh to the two cowmen.

Pick Atherton felt sweat crack on his forehead when he saw how tight her finger was on the trigger. She meant business. There had been nobody in sight when he and Pecos rode up, their attention caught by a wagon on dishing wheels here at the springs. It stood at the old adobe where the Mesa outfit stored stock salt and tools. There was an outdoor fire over there. A grub box and cooking utensils were scattered around it. A couple of ribby horses rummaged on the nearby grass. It was a typical mover's outfit, and this was private range and private water. Then they had discovered her down by the pool of the spring, previously concealed by the depression.

'It happens I have something to say,' Pick said, trying not to look at that trigger finger. 'This is quite a distance from the main trail. You lost or something?'

'We know where we are,' the girl said, 'and we know where we intend to stay.'

So she had expected trouble.

'Here?' Pick said, his gray eyes cooling, growing harder.

The punchers swung their heads. The door of the adobe had cracked open noisily. A man stood framed there, tall, trail-grimed, and looking sleepy. He blinked against the outside glare, yawned, and walked forward to the spring fence. He was a loose-coupled man, long-gaited. A typical shiftless mover, Pick thought. He had seen a lot of them, stopping only long enough to give somebody trouble, then trailing on, the West's equivalent of a gypsy.

'What's the trouble, Piper?' the man said. He had a whiskey voice.

'Something about us being here,' the girl said, nodding at Pick. She seemed to have centered her antipathy in him already. 'He don't act like he likes it.'

Pick meant to be reasonable about this if he could. 'These springs belong to Mesa Ranch,' he said. 'And Mesa Ranch belongs to me. The young lady sort of indicated you're fixing to stay, friend. That would be all right, except I've got cattle that need this water and range. This is dry country. You couldn't have got this deep without finding that out.'

'We found it out.' The mover scratched an ear. 'You're Atherton, I guess. A fellow told me about you. Also that there's a springs in this basin marked with Joshua trees that you claim without a shred of right. Any other springs around here of that description, Atherton?'

'This is Josh Springs,' Pick said. Without the spitfire holding the rifle this man wouldn't be half as insolent. Now he showed a glimmering-eyed assurance. 'Somebody filled you full of hot air, friend. Who was it?'

'A fellow in town.'

'What town?'

'Las Vegas, when we come through the other day. I don't see how that makes any difference.'

Pick's voice lost its mildness. 'It makes a lot of difference. Just who are you, mister?'

The man looked at him with beady eyes. 'The name's Tarrone—Yancy Tarrone. From here and there, up to now. As of now, this is my address.'

Pick nodded grimly. 'I see. It's the first time Wells Packwood's hired a family man to squat on my range for him. That fooled me for a minute, Tarrone. So you're another tool of his. I take it this—uh—lady's your wife?'

The girl's eyes narrowed at the way he asked the question. Pinched lips spoiled a naturally attractive mouth.

'She's my daughter,' Tarrone said. 'The wife's indoors trying to sleep. Like I was before you raised a rumpus out here. I've got a boy bucketing around somewhere, getting acquainted with the country. That makes me a family man, but I don't know what you mean

4

about Packwood putting squatters on your range. I aim to squat, but this here ain't your range.'

'And it's time you got off of it,' Piper said, shifting the rifle. There was none of her father's hangdog quality in her. She'd use the thing promptly if he tried to start them moving down the trail right now as he should.

'I know what Packwood told you,' he said as calmly as he could. 'I only bought Mesa a while back. He takes the stand that the sale only covered the patented land. He says the former owner lacked the power to transfer rights to water on the public range. That's horse sweat. The cow country's nearly all public land. First use establishes a claim that's always been recognized.'

Tarrone's eyes glittered. 'But you never made the first use of these springs, Atherton. Man ahead of you did.'

'All right. I made the second use, which establishes the same rights.'

'You got stuff here now? I don't see it.'

'It's in the mountains summering.'

'Then I'd say these springs are vacant. They sure as hell look that way.'

The argument was specious and Tarrone seemed to know it, so he was probably relying on the power of Packwood's big Clover Leaf outfit to back him here.

'Too bad,' Pick said, 'that you've got a family, because you're biting off a lot more

5

than you can chew. It looks like you've traveled quite a ways, so rest up today. But be gone by morning.'

'Or?'

'I'll move you on, myself.'

'Come over and try it,' the girl said, and her grip tightened again on the rifle.

Pick swung his horse. Pecos rode beside him, and they moved onto the far-reaching flat of the Hueco, deep in the hot country bordering the Amargosa Desert. The hoofs of the horses struck softly on the sandy hot earth. Ahead Eagle Point showed through a pink and violet haze against a low scarp that ran the width of the basin.

Beyond the point rose a higher mesa that lay on a diagonal to the rest. Mesa Ranch used its shade for headquarters. It was a much smaller outfit than it had once been. So was Big Springs, which shared the basin. The losses to Packwood had come before Pick's time, but he wasn't permitting any more of it.

Pecos spoke a thought already coming into Pick's mind. 'What's the matter with Luke Gallatin that makes him tuck his tail the way he does? His old man was willing to fight for Big Springs. Why ain't Luke?'

'For one thing, his old man was killed doing it,' Pick said.

'And that made Luke gun-shy?'

'I think his wife's got something to do with it. He's never said anything, but I sort of got that impression.'

Bitterly Pecos said, 'If Packwood can keep that squatter on Josh, Luke's got to fight or go clean under this time. If he keeps out of it he'll hamstring us.'

Pick agreed. He would have rolled Packwood back already and avoided a situation like this if the other basin outfit had been willing to support him. But Big Springs had lost heavily in the first struggle, and Luke lived in the false hope that by accepting the status quo he could avoid further inroads. That had kept Pick from fighting fire with fire, for he could not take the initiative without reprisals that would affect Big Springs. Now Packwood had made the boldest move of all, putting a squatter in the basin proper. Luke Gallatin would have to fish or cut bait.

An old man sat in the shade at Eagle Point, spindle-trunked and bushy-faced. Sam Masterson was a desert rat who had lived in a shack at the foot of the Drys for thirty years. His crowbait horse stood half asleep in the black shadow of the pinnacle.

'I was heading for Mesa,' Sam said, 'and seen you coming. You must have noticed what lit at Josh Springs.'

'When did you find out?' Pick said.

'Yesterday.' Sam shifted his tobacco from one cheek to the other. 'I seen their dust rolling in and went over for a look. They're a sorry outfit if ever I seen one and plumb set on

7

taking over Josh.'

'I know. And it beats me why Packwood picked that bunch. They're not the hard cases he put on the other water holes, and he knows they'll start a fight.'

'It's his doings,' Sam said, nodding. 'And if you tell me what you aim to do about them, maybe I can tell you why he picked them.'

'I invited them off, and off they go. Tomorrow morning.'

'Better think twice about that. Packwood's gone a long ways with his water grabbing, even for a country mighty shy on law. What he needs is a fighting cause, something to excuse him for keeping on with it. Like protecting that sorry nester family on water it figures it's got some right to.'

Pick frowned. 'I don't get you, Sam.'

'Tarrone ain't much of a specimen,' Sam said, 'but folks'll feel sorry for them women and the boy. Drifters, always on the go, ragged and half starved, following a itchy-footed man around the country. They get a chance to stay put and Mesa drives them off. It's loaded, Pick. Packwood run into that outfit in Las Vegas. He was there last week. He seen just what he needed.'

'You could be right,' Pick said. 'But they can't stay there. He'd only take Josh away from them, himself, when he got ready. And with him on three sides of us we wouldn't have a chance to hold onto the rest.'

8

'I still wouldn't take his bait.'

Sam climbed to his feet and, with a nod, moved off to his horse, a spry man although he was close to eighty. A moment later he rode off across the flat, heading for his shack at Wagon Tire Well.

'The old gopher's right,' Pecos said. 'Hadn't I better stay down till you've got it settled?'

'I can handle it,' Pick said. 'If Packwood's on the move again, they might try something on the steers. You'd better get back to them.'

Pecos had come down the night before for supplies. He'd been headed for the summer range that morning when he saw the new squatter camp from a distance and smoked back to tell Pick. Pecos now got the pack horses he had left at Barrel Spring and resumed his journey. Pick rode on to headquarters, simmering, knowing he had to master the situation without doing what Sam had warned against.

Charlie Gallatin, who established Big Springs, had been killed in the fight with Clover Leaf. Thereupon Mesa's founder, Plez Brown, had seen the writing on the wall and given up. But Brown had fooled Wells Packwood. Instead of taking the man's offer for Mesa, he had gone to Las Vegas hunting an outside buyer. A mutual friend had put him in touch with Pick. Brown was ageing, Pick was young, brash, and tough, and they worked out a mutually advantageous deal. The upset had added disgruntlement to Packwood's ambitions for Mesa. Pick had never entertained the hope that he had given up.

When he had eaten a hurried noon meal, Pick resaddled. Immediately afterward he struck into the canyon leading onto the mesa behind the ranch buildings. A week ago there had been a little band of his horses strayed too close to Clover Leaf. He hadn't had a chance to check on them in several days. With trouble shaping up fast it would be well to do so.

The mesa rose sheer and high on the near side and ran flat and ribby for nearly a mile. Then it fell to the low bench extending on to Clover Leaf's self-proclaimed boundary at the edge of the basin. Stunted juniper and a few nut pines grew in patches where the rocky mesa top caught enough soil. Elsewhere the area sprawled barren and hot. Though degraded by erosion and flaunting acres of rock, the formation was one of the ranch's assets so coveted by Wells Packwood.

The Huecos giving the basin its name were shallow depressions that everywhere caught the rains that fell furiously when they came at all. This was percolated into rocky caverns that, seeping on into the water table, fed springs far about. The process created a supply that Clover Leaf coveted, for in a dry country one good spring could be the key to a vast area of grass.

Pick rode slack in the saddle, following an

old trail in a climbing canyon that cut off miles to Mesa's west range. From the summit of the uplift he could see a section of the Amargosa Desert. Beyond the low Dry range, it ran sear and gray into the haze, its only green a thin streak of mesquite along the wash of an ancient river. He topped over and started down.

Far forward on the lower bench a playa lay athwart a gap by which the wagon road entered the Amargosa and ran on to Long String and the railroad. He couldn't see his horses anywhere short of the playa. It was a good thing he had wondered about them, for he would have to hunt them up and move them closer to headquarters. Thieves worked this lonely country steadily, and all the cattle outfits lost saddle stock each year. There was never any telling what new deviltry would come from Clover Leaf.

He reached the playa, the bed of an ancient lake now white, flat, and crackled. He found the horses at Mesa's outermost water hole on this side of its range. There were only five head where last week, when he saw them, there had been six. Recalling the animals, he realized that a star-faced roan was missing.

He turned south and rode to the barbed-wire fence, one that Clover Leaf had built from the lower end of the playa to the east mountains. Beyond the fence was a wide strip of grass and several good waterings, all seized

11

by Packwood when Plez Brown ran Mesa. Beyond this were the low brown mounds of the Hueco Hills. He rode to a gate due ahead and halted, drifting his eyes across the sand.

A half-shod horse had come through the gate not long ago, entering Mesa range. That in itself wasn't anything to get excited over. Yet the intruder had left again, followed by another and unshod horse. But just one, the starface, when there had been five other good horses that could have been taken at the same time. The gate was now closed, but the tracks were fairly fresh, so he passed through. He shut the gate behind him again and followed the tracks to Clover Leaf's road, which ran between the fence and the hills.

The thief had led the starface into a rut of the road, a trough of loose sand ground up by the wheels of Clover Leaf's buckboard and freight wagon. The sand had already tumbled in until the horse tracks were soon lost, as the thief had expected. Those remaining pointed toward the gap and escape into the vastness beyond it. Running down the fellow would take far more time than Pick could spare at the moment. Someone might hope to draw him into such a chase while Tarrone got dug in at Josh Springs.

He rode back to the gate and had swung down to reopen it when he turned to look to the west. A buggy broke around the end of a mesquite patch, following the road from the gap. He waited, his eyes going hard.

Drawn by a team of trotters, the buggy came on fast. He saw two passengers, and one had the shape of a woman. A moment later he was certain it was Wells Packwood and his wife. Packwood seemed wary but pulled up, scarcely daring to ignore a man so obviously waiting there for him.

Pick had only contempt for the thickset middle-aged rancher but touched his hat to Abby Packwood, who wore a duster and scarf-anchored hat. She had never shown him her husband's animosity, although the smile with which she acknowledged his courtesy was fleet and withdrawn. Except for a cool tip of the head, Packwood made no greeting at all.

'I had a talk with Yancy Tarrone, this morning,' Pick said. 'It seems you sold him a big bill of goods, Packwood.'

Packwood was burly, hard, and insulated, of much coarser fiber than his wife. There was a look of brute force in his face and in the way he handled himself. He was discomfited having his wife hear this, but he made no attempt to cover up by denying a connection with Tarrone.

'They're shirttail relatives of a friend of mine,' he said curtly. 'Hunting land. What's wrong with me telling them about Josh Springs? You don't own them and never will.'

'I know your argument on that point.' Pick's voice was heavy, carrying. It made Abby

13

Packwood look up at him. 'And I don't believe it a bit more than you do. But Tarrone's swallowed it or seems to have. That was a skunk's trick on your part.'

Anger tightened Packwood's face. 'I wouldn't give them trouble, Atherton. Since I've sponsored them, I'll protect them.'

'Till they've served your stinking purpose,' Pick said bitterly. 'I want you to know I understand the caper, Packwood. You're after Josh Springs now and you're using those folks outrageously.'

For the first time Abby Packwood seemed to understand and be concerned. She was dark, slender, much younger than Packwood. Pick had sensed before that she was unhappy. The other neighborhood women avoided her because of her husband. She started to speak to Packwood, then reconsidered. She looked away toward the Piutes, whose peaks burned with sunlight, their canyons drowned in shadow.

'We'll talk about it another time,' Packwood said. 'My wife's tired and wants to get home.' He flicked the whip, and the buggy ran on.

14

CHAPTER TWO

After a lonely supper Pick saddled a horse from the trap and rode east over the wild-rye meadow. It was eight miles to Big Springs, yet he traveled without hurry. The day's heat still lay on the land, but little reduced in the dusk. High in the Piutes the last sun blazed across the peaks. The closer ranges tumbled in darkening masses, and the timber, where the last light struck, blazed in a gold-washed green.

The Gallatin ranch buildings were at the foot of these mountains in a grove of old cottonwood. They were mostly adobe, the long ranch house, a stable, and the bunkhouse that once in busy seasons had housed a dozen riders. Barbed-wire corrals and traps added a more modern note, as did a wind pump that wailed on its tower.

Luke Gallatin stood in the yard when Pick rode in. Mike Terry, his one remaining puncher, motioned a greeting from the bunkhouse steps but remained seated. He had a piece of wood in one hand, a jackknife in the other.

'Well howdy, Pick,' Luke said. 'You're night-owling. What's up?'

He was around thirty, a silent man slow to warm to strangers and still not wholly at ease with the rough new owner of Mesa. He and Mike were baching it now, Pick knew, his wife being away on a visit to her folks. They had been married in Rhyolite, where she had taught school, but he understood that she had grown up on the Coast. Her absence gave him a chance to get down to cases with Luke, something that was badly needed.

'Somebody made off with that starface of mine,' Pick said. 'You better be on the lookout for more of the same on your range. But I came over mainly about Packwood. He's put a drifter on Josh Springs. I guess you know what that means. He couldn't pick up a better jumping-off place against you and me.'

'Him again,' Luke said with a groan.

'This time he picked a family man. He told me this afternoon he intends to protect them. Sam Masterson thinks he wants me to drive them off to stir up resentment against me. Kind of a smoke screen for what Packwood wants to pull off for himself.'

'That's got his trade-mark,' Luke said worriedly. 'But what else is there to do about it?'

'Maybe there's something Packwood didn't figure on,' Pick said. 'It struck me this evening I might be able to buy off Tarrone. He's the new squatter and he's no stayer. For enough dinero he might be glad to roll on and avoid a fight. It's worth a try, and I'm going there from here to see.'

16

Luke flung an uneasy glance toward his old rider. In a murmur he said, 'Come over to the porch.'

Realizing he wanted to get out of earshot, Pick followed him to the vine-covered gallery of the house.

There Luke said, 'Mike's got a bad enough opinion of me as it is. And I expect you have. My dad was murdered by Clover Leaf, even if they did stand together and put him in the wrong in that gun fight. They're holding a lot of range that belongs to me now. They keep rubbing my nose in it. But—well, Pick, I'm kind of helpless. Olive just doesn't see things the way I do.'

Rebellion was close to the surface in the man. Pick knew that Luke was the one who needed to do the talking. He said nothing.

'My father was killed the day after we were married,' Luke resumed. 'We were still in Rhyolite. The way I took it scared her half to death. She made me promise not to retaliate, which I was swearing to do, before she'd come home with me to live. She'd still rather we lived somewhere else. And she's got a point. This damned country brings out the worst in people. Every critter on the desert has got to kill or be killed. A man can't blame a woman for hating it.'

'You're speaking her piece, Luke. I'd rather hear yours.'

The rebellion broke through then. Hotly

17

Luke said, 'All right, you'll hear it. I want Big Springs to be the ranch my father made it. I want to see Wells Packwood and Pierce Hannegan pay for killing him. I want what I wanted the day it happened and I never stopped wanting it. But I love my wife, Pick. I know how she feels. She—hell, if getting killed was all it amounted to. There's something I dread worse. Losing her. I made a promise she won't let me out of, and if I broke it that's what would happen.'

'You'll have to make your stand pretty soon, Luke,' Pick said grimly. He turned to leave, then swung back. 'And there's something she might be wrong about. There's times when this country brings out the best in people, too. I hope she finds it out.'

He rode on, taking a northwesterly direction for about three miles. Thereafter he lifted the speed of the horse and traveled west under a ceiling of emerging stars. Finally he slanted to the right once more, nearing the pitching ranges of the Sapphires that rose behind a pinpoint of light. The light was the little storage building at Josh Springs now being occupied by the Tarrones.

He was following along the lava crop east of the springs when, at a slowed gait, he caught the impact of a distant sound in the night. Reining in, he sat with a checked breath, his ears keened in concern. The sound came again, a rattling rain registering in his ears. It

18

was gunfire. The extent drew the lines of his face into a worried set. There was shooting at Josh Springs.

He raked his spurs and sent his horse streaking forward through the night. The light at the springs had been extinguished by then. The adobe was under a bristling attack. His only thought at the moment was to break it up. He jerked up his six-gun and whipped a shot forward to let them know he was coming. The drum of his horse's hoofs also registered up there. The shooting stopped, then after a lull there were two final shots. A pair of riders cut away from the springs. They meant to lose themselves in the deeper obscurity along the brushy base of the foothills, he saw.

He sprang his horse onto the gravel slope with its desert brush and the rubble that helped cover them. By then his thoughts had sorted themselves out. The forward riders were his own enemies. They intended to make the attack on the Tarrones look like it had come from Mesa. He flung another angry shot as he pursued them, drawing two in reply. He pushed headlong, not shooting again but trying to press them into a bay in the forward foot slope and trap them.

They caught onto his intention and worked farther south, managing to keep the gap between from shortening. He continued to crowd them. He might still drive them close enough to Wagon Tire Well, where Sam

Masterson lived, to arouse the old desert rat. Sam had a head like a needle and would guess what was happening. Pick knew how desperately he would need support in his account of the shoot-up of the squatter family. Unless he could clear himself, Packwood would have the outrage he wanted.

The quarry did no more firing but lent themselves to guiding their rushing horses in and out of the scattered cover. Minutes passed and the pattern remained unchanged. Then all at once the two ahead swung west. Pick realized that they were making for Live Oak Canyon. It would take them deep into the Drys where he could not follow in the night without risk of a fatal deadfall. Yet he stayed on their heels until, with a flurry of parting shots, they vanished into the black blotch of the canyon.

He reined in his hard-driven horse still two miles short of Wagon Tire. He hated to return to Josh Springs, for he failed to see how the adobe could have undergone that storm of bullets without somebody's being hit. After resting his horse a moment and reloading his gun, he headed back to face it.

The adobe was still dark. Pick hailed it loudly, urgently, as he drew close. For a moment there was no answer, then a rifle sped its crash across the night. He saw the flash, either at the window or in the doorway. The bullet sought him in dead earnestness, and he hastily pulled up his horse.

He sent his voice ringing forward. 'Hold it. I'm a friend.'

The voice that hurled back to him was tight, but he knew it was Piper's. 'Who is it?'

'Pick Atherton from Mesa.'

The answer was another shot that made him duck his head. More words came shrilly to him.

'You killed Pa. It's a wonder you didn't kill all of us, damn you.'

'That wasn't me, Piper,' he shouted back. 'I only drove them off. I want to help you. Let me come in.'

Two more shots punched out. He knew she would never believe him, that only a few ever would. He pulled back, convinced that she would shoot him down if he tried to go in regardless. He was about to turn away when, over against the back fence of the corral at the springs, he saw a shape on the ground. He wanted a look but dared not ride in that close to the adobe. He went on to the cover of the lava rock, where he swung down and left the horse. Keeping the old wagon between himself and the hostile adobe, he moved back carefully and came to the wire fence.

The shape on the ground was a horse, saddled, and there was starlight to show him it was the missing star face. It was shot through the head. It had been stolen and brought here intentionally. The attackers had killed it before fleeing to pin the guilt on Mesa Ranch.

21

A dead horse was impossible to move or burn or bury without a lot of time and work.

Man, you're in trouble, Pick told himself. They've got you where they want you already . . .

Maybe. The panic left. His conscience was clear. He would call in the law himself, state the facts, and stand on them.

It was a thirty-mile ride to Long String, the nearest telegraph office. He started immediately, heading first for Wagon Tire Well. He had taken a lot out of his horse and would have liked a fresh one, yet begrudged the time required to return to the ranch. Sam had nothing but a scrawny old saddler and a burro he used on his prospects in the desert. But Pick wanted to tell him what had happened and have him go over to the Tarrones'. Sam had been there before, and the terrified girl might let him come in. He reached the shack in the cottonwoods along the spring seepage, hallooing the old prospector out of his bunk.

'I never heard a thing,' Sam said dismally when he had been informed. 'But you're dead right. That was Clover Leaf's doing. They had plenty of chance to pick up and hide your starface till they needed it.'

'That was pure murder,' Pick said, his voice heavy with anger. 'They didn't care who they hit, whether they killed him or didn't. When it gets around, there'll be a lynching party after me for it.'

Sam nodded somberly. 'That dead horse will be hard to explain. Did you mention to anybody beforehand that it had been stolen? That'd help you. You sure couldn't have known beforehand it would be shot in the fracas.'

'I went over and told Luke Gallatin.'

Sam groaned. 'And he's too damned chickenhearted to back you against Packwood.'

'I'm not so sure, Sam. But I've got to get riding.'

'Yeah. Get at it.'

Pick sped down the basin toward the gap. He went through the gate in the fence Reedy Smith, a Clover Leaf squatter, had built. It ran from the Drys to the playa to hold Mesa stock off range, that Smith had grabbed from Brown with Packwood's help. He passed within shouting distance of the squatter's shack, tempted to stop and see if Smith was home or with the party that had vanished into the Drys. Urgency decided him against it. Soon afterward he rushed by another squatter setup and entered the gap, following the wagon trail.

Afterward he crowded his horse steadily through the desert darkness. Gaining perspective, he began to feel the plight of the girl he had seen dancing by the spring pond only that morning. The trail dust had been cleansed from her body, her woman's

23

daintiness had been restored. In her heart had been a hope that she never again would roll on in the dish-wheeled old wagon. That had been behind the soft smile, the dreaminess he now remembered.

He wondered what their decision would be, if they would now give up and hit the trails that led nowhere. He remembered her will, the fire in her eyes, the steel in her stance. It was more likely that she would try to stay at Josh Springs. Clover Leaf would encourage her to do it. However appealing a girl in a country that held so few, she would be his enemy. She had proved that tonight. She had tried earnestly to kill him.

CHAPTER THREE

Piper sagged against the doorjamb, the rifle hanging down in her trembling hand. The brown back of the other hand was pressed to her forehead, and for a moment she closed her eyes. She heard the rasp of her mother's dry sob and straightened. Her eyes opened upon a world she knew to be changed forever. And it was changed for the worse, no matter how impossible that had seemed only days before.

'Don't strike a light, Rip,' Piper said.

Her brother had picked up a lantern. He put it down. He had come up beside the woman kneeling on the ground and the man stretched there so unmoving. Rip said, 'They're gone now.'

'Maybe and maybe not.'

She studied the dark desert out past the wagon. Rip's and her beds were there under the wagon, kicked apart when they scrambled out as the first shots rattled the night. Her father and mother had retired to sleep in the soddy. She would never forget her father pitching headlong from the doorway where he had appeared with the rifle. That had released a ferocity in her she only then knew she possessed.

Bullets had laced the air thickly, yet she had run across. She swept up the rifle from her father's released grip and sprang up the steps for better vision. But before she could get her bearings and find a target the shooting quit. She had heard horses depart hurriedly. Then silence came back to the night.

Piper went down the steps and put her hand gently on her mother's sharp shoulder blade.

'Is he—?'

Her mother nodded. Her reply was a moan shaped into words. 'Oh, what will we do, Piper? What will we do now?'

Piper knew that the question was not intended to be answered. It was one to which there was none. But Rip, a large, solemn boy for his sixteen years, shifted his feet and tried. He said in a tight way, 'We'll get along, Ma. We'll go on someplace where I can find a job. Maybe a stable job in some town.'

'We're staying here,' Piper said. Her voice was very quiet and very sure.

It was a spontaneous choice, but she knew at once that there could be no other. For the first time in her memory her father had been willing to settle somewhere to stay. The man he had met in Las Vegas had enthused him with talk of raising beef for mining camps. He had mentioned giving them cattle to run on shares. No one had offered Yancy Tarrone so much before. His skeptical family had finally succumbed to his infectious cheer.

Her mother got a bed blanket and covered him. She said finally in a dull voice, 'Stay here,

26

Piper? After this?'

'Anything Pa could do I can do, and Rip can help me.'

'It's clean out of the question. We'll have to do what Rip said, I reckon.'

Piper hardly heard as she turned and walked out toward the wagon. The horse travel had drained into the far night. Perhaps she should feel grief for her father, but she did not. Her reaction was shock, fear, and fury, but not sorrow. Her father had not been kind to them. He had not come here out of consideration for them at all. He had spent a lifetime hunting the big chance. He had thought it was here, that was all. And maybe it was here for her. She was in too great a turmoil to wonder if there was a hidden motive in Packwood's benevolence. Maybe she could convince him she could run a small cattle outfit herself.

She saw something dark and obscure out by the spring fence. Her heart contracted. She decided that the object was too large to be a hiding man and made herself walk toward it. Presently she could tell that it was a downed horse, dead or badly injured. She came up to it cautiously, able to see in the thin sky light the white star on its forehead.

She hurried to the camp and got matches, then went back to the horse. A brief light showed her its M brand. A grim satisfaction came to her, not from confirming that Mesa had attacked them because they had rejected

27

its ultimatum in advance. The dead horse would convict Atherton and his puncher. There would be no more of tonight's kind of terror. They would be able to stay here at Josh Springs. Her relief was tremendous.

She considered the tall, hard-faced Atherton, to whom she had taken an intense dislike on sight. Since she was about twelve, men had offended her with their callous, trespassing eyes. She was a mover's daughter, shabby, hopeless, and poor. Some of them had tried to lay more on her than their hot eyes, considering it appropriate to her. She had seen no such lust in the faces of Atherton and his companion. But she didn't for a minute believe they had just come up when she discovered them. The thought of their watching her silly dancing was bad enough. Before that she had bathed, unabashedly stripped because there seemed to be no one but her family within miles. It made her feel that she had stupidly pandered to their low pleasure. That they had let her was the measure of their respect for her.

She was moving back to the camp when a sound of travel in the outer night struck her ears. She hastened on and found her mother and Rip still standing awkwardly over her father's body.

'Somebody's coming,' she said quietly. 'Get indoors.'

'Not again,' her mother said. She sounded

less alarmed than tired.

'I'll take care of it, Ma. Hurry.'

She got the rifle and stood inside the soddy doorway, her family behind her, and listened to the hoofbeat grow stronger in the silent night. Afterward somebody hailed them. She didn't act until a rider emerged out of the darkness and came stubbornly on. Then she lifted the rifle, aimed carefully, and fired.

A shout fell across the night. 'Hold it. I'm a friend.'

She asked who it was, and when he said Atherton she knew it was a trick. She shot again, then sent her accusing screams hurtling to him. His denial, his pretense of help made her fire twice more and he was gone. She stood shaken afterward, disturbed by how badly she had wanted to kill him.

'Maybe he told the truth,' her mother said dubiously at last. 'Packwood's offer sounded too good to me to be true. Who does all that for strangers without a profit on it? Especially for people like us.'

'Hah,' Piper said.

'Well, I ain't jumping to conclusions. We could have been played for fools.'

'Go look at the M brand on that dead horse out there,' Piper said.

Her mother fell silent. Pick Atherton's departing horse grew inaudible in the desert distance. The tensions wrought by his reappearance loosened and queerly made her

29

want to cry. Maybe it was because her mother had dragged one small speck of doubt into her mind. She didn't want to lose the certitude that let her hate so solidly. She didn't want to give up the hope that Packwood might still help her.

Later, when another rider came in, she felt no great alarm. She had seen the slow-moving horse and its high figure the day before. She knew it was the old prospector even before he identified himself. Her reaction turned into relief, for he had seemed harmless and reliable yesterday.

Sam Masterson rode into the camp and swung out of the saddle with an agility that surprised her. She liked the way he removed his hat when he glanced down at the figure on the ground. Then he looked at her mother and his face was gentle and sad.

'I'm right sorry, ma'am. Figured I might be able to help a little, by your leave.'

'How'd you know about it so soon?' Rip said in a blurt.

'Pick Atherton stopped to tell me. Asked me to come over. He's on his way to wire the sheriff.'

'The sheriff?' Piper said with a gasp.

Sam's head turned her way. He said gently, 'He's got to be fetched in a case like this.'

'I know that. But Atherton—why, they're the ones who did it.'

Sam shook his head. 'No, ma'am. Like I

30

tried to tell your pa yesterday. You folks have got the wrong idea of things. Pick couldn't prove it yet, but it's mighty likely it was Clover Leaf that shot you up. Packwood's outfit. The man you thinks a friend.'

'There's a dead Mesa horse out past the spring.'

'Stolen off of Mesa. Pick discovered that yesterday.'

'Very, very likely,' Piper said.

Sam shrugged. He looked at Rip and said kindly, 'Son, we'd best tote your daddy indoors.' Rip nodded, and they moved Yancy Tarrone's body inside. They came out, closing the door, and Sam said, 'There won't be any more trouble tonight, and it's getting cold. I'll light a fire.'

Piper trusted him completely, except for his excusing of Mesa. She watched him kindle the fire, saw it strengthen. His presence was a comfort for, old as he was, he seemed surprisingly capable. And something better, he seemed extraordinarily kind and considerate. She had known prospectors and punchers, miners and freighters. Now she acknowledged that some of them, a very few; could be like that. He made coffee, then required them to drink it, and it made them feel better.

Sam talked matter-of-factly as he moved about. The county seat was Tonopah, which was quite a way off. If there was no delay in reaching him, the sheriff could be in Long

31

String on the next day's train. He had been in the basin before, Sam said. This wasn't its first trouble and was not apt to be its last. Sunderleaf, the sheriff, was a completely honest man and would try to get to the bottom of things.

The old man talked of prospecting. That caught Rip's interest and turned his thoughts away from the night's bloody violence, as Sam probably intended. Piper walked out under the stars, unable to surrender her own mind. She was trying hard to believe that Sam was simply biased in Atherton's favor. Certainly he had not been a witness to the things that excused Mesa. He only had Atherton's own account.

Whatever, Packwood had offered help that she still wanted. Atherton had ordered them to be on their way under threat of moving them by force. She had been aware of the contempt in his eyes when he regarded her father. She was her father's own flesh, a mover girl, a gypsy without a gypsy's colorfulness and pleasure in the nomadic life. She and Rip would have been illiterate if her mother hadn't made them study even when they couldn't be in a school . . .

Again sound drummed its signal across the deepening night. The oncomers moved boldly across the flat basin floor, as Sam had, and she thought there were three of them. She hurried back to the camp to find Sam on his feet, listening intently and staring out into the

32

desert. His frown alarmed her.

'Who'd they be?' she said in a tight voice.

'Dunno, miss. They come along the Drys. Packwood's got some squatters along there. It could be somebody from Clover Leaf.'

To her surprise, that did nothing to ease her tension, even when the arrivers called forward reassuringly before they rode in. Sam kept to his feet and he still looked wary, uneasy. The trio that rode up took a quick, hard look at him, too. They were all punchers, rough, aggressive-looking men.

'Howdy, Sam,' the biggest one said tartly. The old man said nothing, and the speaker looked at Mrs. Tarrone. 'Evening, ma'am. Is the mister around?'

'Pierce Hannegan,' Sam said in a voice heavy with dislike, 'you know damned well this camp couldn't be shot up the way it was without somebody being hurt or killed. Somebody was killed. Tarrone. Murdered by your Clover Leaf night riders.'

'Shot up?' Hannegan straightened and put a flat stare on the oldster. 'What are you talking about?'

'We were attacked tonight,' Piper said. 'My father was killed.'

'Well, I'm not surprised,' Hannegan said, swinging out of the saddle. 'Packwood met Atherton on the road today, and Atherton threatened you people. Packwood was coming in from Long String and I was down in the hills

33

with the boys, so he couldn't get in touch with me right off. But he wanted somebody here to look out for you folks after Atherton's talk. I'm sure sorry we couldn't get here sooner.'

'A likely yarn,' Sam said with a snort. He turned away.

Hannegan was middle-aged but vigorous and powerful. His hard eyes swung to Piper, then to her mother. In a voice meant to be gentle he said, 'This old coot's harmless, but you better know he's cracked. Lived too long with no company but a burro, I guess. They all go crazy in time, and he's had time. He was here ahead of the Indians.'

Sam swung back, bristling, then he shrugged.

Piper looked at Hannegan in surprise. There was serenity in the way he talked, and he made sense, accounting for Sam's support of Mesa. Yet it bothered her to think of the old man as being off in the head. That didn't ring true to her.

'Mr. Masterson's been mighty kind,' she said, surprised that her voice carried heat. 'And we appreciate it.'

Frowning at Sam, Hannegan said, 'You better go home and get some sleep. Me and the boys'll take care of things here.' He turned and motioned to his punchers. One caught the reins of the ramrod's horse and led it off toward the spring. The other went along. Piper saw them loosen the saddle cinches and put on hobbles. They meant to stay whether or not they were asked, and this gave her a queer quirk of annoyance.

Her mother also sensed that trouble was about to erupt between Hannegan and Sam. She said, 'We're mighty obliged to you for coming over, Mr. Masterson. They seem to be staying, so you might as well get your rest.'

Sam shrugged and walked out to his nag.

Hannegan went to the fire and poured a cup of coffee. He stood with his thick legs spread while he drank it. The punchers came in and likewise helped themselves to the coffee. Piper felt a deep uneasiness she had not noticed when the old man had been the only outsider there. Hannegan seemed indifferent to them now, interested only in being there with his men.

Her mother said, 'We might as well try to rest, Piper. You come too, Rip.'

They went out to the wagon.

Later, lying wide-eyed beside her mother under the wagon, Piper watched the men at the fire. They weren't talking much but seemed to have taken an assured possession of the camp. Her head ached from trying to make sense out of the charges and countercharges. Her mother was right about the unlikelihood of kindness coming out of men like those toward the Tarrones. Yet the Mesa men had struck her as being equally indurated and self-interested. They were all like the country that

35

supported them. Everything had been dried out of them but ferocity. She would have to be that way herself and could be. She had felt it already that night.

Without awareness of being drowsy, she opened her eyes to find the night gone. She heard her mother's steady breathing and lifted her head to see Rip asleep under the other end of the wagon. She felt tired and vulnerable and all at once completely uncertain. Her father had been a man. Right or wrong, selfish or not, he had made the decisions and met their responsibilities in his makeshift way. Now he was dead.

She glanced toward the camp and saw only one man there. Checking in the other direction, she saw only two of their horses. They apparently were doing a service, and she supposed she ought to fix their breakfast. She felt strongly disinclined to do so. She slipped out of the blankets, combed her hair with her fingers, and moved unseen to the spring. She washed her hot face and sat while the air dried it, no longer thinking, just trying to ease up.

She was unaware that anyone had come up until she turned her bead suddenly. One of Hannegan's punchers stood grinning at her. She jumped quickly to her feet. He had one of the camp kettles and was after water.

'Another hot day coming,' he said. 'Sheriff better get here fast. Your old man'll be smelling in a day or two of this.'

The coarseness raked across her nerves like a spur. 'How did you know Atherton went to wire him?' she said.

The man stared at her. 'Atherton?'

'He left for the railroad last night. I wondered how you knew.'

The man seemed puzzled. 'I didn't. Hannegan sent Roscoe back to the ranch. The boss'll send for the sheriff.' He came a step closer, that nervous grin still on his homely face. 'Say, you're even better-looking in daylight. That's more'n a man can say about some of you fillies.'

Disgust filled her, and she knew she hated both sides in the bitter conflict raging in this basin. They would have to roll on again, taking the trail to nowhere, depending on Rip, who would become like their father. She turned and fled toward the wagon.

CHAPTER FOUR

His telegram filed to the Tonopah sheriff, Pick walked out of the depot into the dawnburst over the desert. Aggressive light burned over the ranges and consumed the last of the night. Long String at any hour was a drab desert hamlet on the Tonopah and Tidewater railroad, which came in through the wastes from the coast and vanished on into Nevada. Cottonwood and mesquite drove their roots into some underground water supply, greening the town, making it habitable to the inured and hardy. Freighters based there and prospectors came in from the canyons for supplies, as did scattered dry-country ranchers.

Pick went to his horse, trying to think ahead. A deep uneasiness remained in him, a thorough distrust of the situation in which Clover Leaf had caught him. In trying to help Piper he had declared his identity boldly in the night. That impulsive kindness could well be his complete ruin. It placed him there at Josh Springs with the dead Mesa horse, after ordering the Tarrones to leave the springs or be removed by force.

His fatigue came down on him crushingly. As he glanced at the horse he knew it was equally dinked, but he had to get back to Mesa without resting. The thought struck him that he could turn off onto the back slope of the Sapphires when he had recrossed the desert. Thus he would reach Mesa's summer camp much sooner than he could return to the home ranch. It would be well to tell his punchers what was going on. He could eat there and catch some sleep. He watered the horse at the trough in front of the livery barn, which was still locked. He stepped tiredly into the saddle and rode out of town.

Before him as he traveled lay a world of sepia sand, greasewood, and cactus. Lizards lived there with horned toads and rattlesnakes, with few other creatures to contest their domain. And yet, far forward and far to the rear, snow peaks rose on the spring range and the lofty Sierras. They meant stored water, forever in view and forever denied the desert.

He narrowed his eyes in a desert man's pucker and moved steadily for several hours, coming finally to the creosote green of the gravel slope under the Sapphires. Both he and the horse picked up a little energy as they climbed out of the furnace heat. They topped the divide and reached Mesa's camp soon afterward. He watered the horse, put it on grass, and stretched out under a nut pine. He was asleep instantly.

Pecos Benton and Blackie Chase, coming in at noon, woke him while trying to avoid it. Their easy greetings puzzled him until he remembered groggily that they didn't know about the murder of Tarrone. Sitting on his heels, Blackie was building a fire in the ashes under the camp kettles. Beyond was a tent fly, stretched on poles, with their beds and extra supplies. Pick rubbed the sleep from his hot eyes and stared at them.

Pecos said, 'Well, sleepyhead. You must've been over to see the drifter girl last night. I figured your threat to run them off was a sandy. To keep me and Blackie away from her, naturally.'

'If you want to trade places,' Pick said irritably, 'you've got a deal. Night riders shot up their camp last night. They killed Tarrone. They left our starface there shot through the head. If you're so blamed smart, add that up.'

The grin faded from Pecos' weathered face. Blackie's eyes pinched narrow. 'Packwood sure tailored that one to fit you,' Blackie said. 'Like a five-hundred-dollar coffin.'

Pecos gave him a glare, no longer amused, and they both went thoughtful. They were young, reckless, and tough, but they had their share of intelligence and understood the gravity of the situation. Pecos was the taller of the pair. One look at Blackie's hair and eyes showed where he got his nickname. There was stew in the kettle, a potent brew in the pot, and both were soon hot. Pick was hungry for the first time in hours and filled his plate. Afterward they sat moodily with coffee and cigarettes, discussing the situation and finding

40

no encouragement in it. Then Pick saddled a fresh horse, left his jaded mount, and rode on for the home ranch.

When he came out of the mountain above the basin floor he swung west, following the screened slope until he had a clear view of Josh Springs. Reined in, he looked at the two Clover Leaf horses, unsaddled but hobbled, on the nearby grass. His mouth pulled long and his eyes smoldered. It was outrageous for Packwood to lend his so-called help to the bereaved family. The Tarrones' allowing Clover Leaf to be there at all proved Sam had not been able to convince them of the truth.

This roweled through Pick when he rode back into the canyon and climbed to a higher elevation. Circumventing the springs, he dropped down in about an hour at Wagon Tire Well.

Sam was enormously angry. 'They've got you jobbed,' he said. 'Hannegan come over to the springs with some men while I was there. He said Packwood was worried about a threat you made against Tarrone. He sent Hannegan over. It was their first chance to see if anybody got hit and what the Tarrones thought.'

'I knew you never got anywhere. Clover Leaf's still holding the place down.'

Sam snorted. 'That double-dealing son told them I was cracked. The frame of mind the Tarrones are in, they probably believe it. Son, Packwood's seized and occupied your best water and made you the one who stands to pay for the killing. If I was you I'd lay low till I had a chance to see the sheriff. The way that outfit works, they might run you down and kill you and claim they were only trying to take you and hold you for the law. That would button the thing up proper for Packwood.'

'I'm not asking for trouble,' Pick said, 'and I'm not dodging it, Sam. Thanks for the help.'

'Such as it was,' Sam said grumpily.

Pick clung to the foothills until he could get onto the bench. Thus he came in behind Eagle Point and took the notch down to the ranch buildings. He turned the horse into the big pasture and walked onto the shady gallery of the old adobe house. He knew Sam was right, that Clover Leaf might start hunting him on its own hook, but he meant to be available when Sheriff Sunderleaf got there. That could be any time or days yet, so he would take the chances he had to take until then.

He had reached the door when a voice inside stopped him motionless. 'Easy, Pick. It's me—Luke.'

Letting out his breath, Pick walked on inside. Luke Gallatin stepped out from the wall against which he had pressed himself. His face was grim and his eyes carried temper.

'I hid my horse behind the house,' Luke said. 'Heard you coming but couldn't see who it was.'

'So the news got over your way.'

42

Luke nodded. 'Packwood sent a man to the telegraph station on the Las Vegas line to wire Sunderleaf. Mike bumped into him, and the fellow told him what they accuse you of doing. Mike lost his temper. He blurted out about you telling us the starface was stolen before the shooting happened. Packwood knows that by now. It gives him a chance to find a way to offset it before Sunderleaf gets here. I figured I'd better let you know.'

'I was counting on that to get me off the hook,' Pick said dismally. 'I'd have had to go straight to Josh after leaving your house, and you know I wasn't riding the starface. Even if I had been I wouldn't have known it would be killed in the shoot-up. So I'd have no reason to tell you it was stolen if it hadn't been.'

'I know, and that still stands in your favor. But Packwood can claim me and Mike are lying to help you out of the jam. He can have a couple of men swear they saw you on that horse that same evening. Just the same, we'll do all we can to clear you.'

'You wouldn't have to,' Pick said thoughtfully. 'And if you do you're buying into the same ruckus I'm in.'

Luke's eyes went smoky. 'You mean you think I'd stoop that low?'

'No. I'm thinking of what you told me about your wife.'

'If Olive'd have me rat out of helping an innocent man clear himself, we might as well

43

call it quits right now.'

'All right. I told Sunderleaf I'd be here. I'll tell him the straight of it and send him to check it.'

'I'm staying here till he shows.'

'No need.'

'There's plenty. Clover Leaf's set up an excuse to ride you down. They're apt to try it.'

Pick shook his head. 'I was scared of that, too. But Packwood must have been jolted when he learned you might prove his evidence against me false. He might not want to take another dangerous step right now.'

'Just the same I'm siding you till Sunderleaf comes.'

'Then let's have some coffee. I'm a little behind on my sleep.'

It was heartening to know that Luke was through with his temporizing and ready to make an open, defiant stand against the powerful Clover Leaf. That wouldn't have been an easy choice, for it meant throwing his wife into the pot along with the ranch already endangered. He hoped that Olive would come to her senses once she understood how things were.

They made coffee and drank it, talking about Nate Sunderleaf. Nye County was huge and there was a chance that he had been away from the county seat when the telegram reached Tonopah. By the time he arrived Packwood could have figured out a way to

44

rectify his plans. Pick could not anticipate the coming days with anything but a wearing dread.

They waited through the last hours of a broiling afternoon with nothing happening. They ate a meal and watched darkness run in and finally shook down for the night. Pick came awake a down times to listen closely and knew that Luke was doing the same. Yet morning came without trouble from Clover Leaf. They knew that Packwood had been given pause by what Mike Terry let slip. So there was a little good in that inadvertency.

While they ate a hasty breakfast, Luke surprised Pick by saying, 'I know you've always felt that way, but I'm sick, too, of only trying to hold my own. I want Big Springs to be the outfit it was before Packwood come up through the hills and stole part of it. When you bought Mesa you bought rights to the range that once went with it. That's unwritten law but recognized by the courts.'

'You mean we ought to carry the fight to Packwood?'

Luke's eyes flashed. 'I always thought so. You're a more experienced fighting man, but I'm telling you I'll back you to the limit if you want to take the initiative away from him.'

That was indeed a change. Pick felt a weight lift from his mind. 'For that we'd need more men than we have,' he said.

'Hire as many as you need, and I'll foot my

share of the bill. By that I don't mean I won't do my share of the fighting, too.'

'If I can stay out of jail, Luke, you've got a deal.'

Nate Sunderleaf arrived at noon. To Pick's relief, he came to Mesa without a Clover Leaf escort. The peace officer nodded somberly and said, 'I don't mind telling you I don't like this visit, boys.'

'You must have seen Packwood already,' Pick said.

'I got a wire from him, too. He made some serious charges, Pick.'

'I expect. Have you been to Josh Springs?'

Sunderleaf nodded. 'Just come from there. I'm sending the body to Rhyolite. The Tarrones are going with it. Hannegan's escorting them. He says his men'll look out for their interests while they're gone.' It was hard to tell if there was irony in the sheriff's voice, and he kept a poker face.

'Their interests,' Pick said bitterly. 'You ought to know that's a blind for grabbing the springs for Clover Leaf. You know the history of this basin.'

Sunderleaf stared at him. 'What have you got to say about that dead horse with your iron?'

'Ask Luke,' Pick said.

'It was stolen before the shooting,' Luke said. 'Pick was over to Big Springs earlier that same evening to warn me about horse thieves.

46

Mike Terry's a witness to that. Sunderleaf, Packwood's men picked up that horse and used it to frame Pick.'

'You say that, but can you prove it?' Sunderleaf said with a frown.

'The circumstances prove it. You knew my dad. You remember how he was killed. I never did think you really believed Hannegan shot him in self-defense.'

'That's one case,' the sheriff said. 'This is another. Packwood's wire said Pick threatened Tarrone. That right, Pick?'

'Not exactly,' Pick said. 'I told Tarrone to get going, but the deadline I set hadn't come when they were attacked. Wouldn't I wait to see what they were going to do before I got rough?'

'I'd be a hard man to sell the idea you'd kill somebody there deliberately. But I understand Tarrone defied you, knocked your warning aside. So a few shots thrown their way might make them reconsider.'

Pick shrugged. Sunderleaf asked more questions, some of them calculated and tricky, but Pick answered frankly in each case. Then the sheriff rode on, heading south into the murky haze. That meant he was going to Clover Leaf next to see Packwood in person.

'Anyway,' Luke said without much cheer, 'he never arrested you as fast as Packwood hoped at first.'

'That doesn't mean he won't on his way

47

back,' Pick said grimly. 'And he seemed pretty suspicious to me.'

'Packwood's made charges he's got to consider.' Luke looked thoughtfully at the ground. 'Well, I'll have to get along. I've got to meet the evening train in Long String.'

'My gosh,' Pick said. 'Why didn't you say so? Is Olive coming home?'

Luke nodded, and Pick knew he was dreading the meeting and what he would have to explain. Luke saddled and rode out across the range toward Big Springs. He would have to hurry now to make Long String in time for the train.

There were chores around the home ranch needing Pick's attention, also. He was leaving the house for the corral when a distant sound arrested him. Paused in the yard, he realized that a horse was coming out of the notch from the high mesa. The slow pace suggested furtiveness, and he turned and walked back to the porch, himself become wary. A moment later the horse emerged from the notch, moving at a quiet walk. His gaze fixed; for a woman rode it, and she looked like Abby Packwood.

It was she, and she came on steadily toward the house. He showed himself as she entered the yard, puzzled and bewildered by her appearance there for the first time since he had lived at Mesa. There was a marked uneasiness on her face, an uncertainty that gave her somewhat the look of moving in her sleep. He removed his hat as she stopped before him, saying nothing to her.

'This isn't treachery,' she said in a heavy voice. 'My husband would think so, but you needn't.'

Again he said nothing.

'May I step onto the gallery?' she said. 'I'm not sure I wasn't followed.'

He nodded silently, perplexed, and she came down. He led her horse into the shade of the house where it wouldn't readily be noticed from a distance. He took her onto the long covered gallery where she dropped into a chair.

'I had to come,' she said. Her eyes searched his face, and in them was a beseeching look, a mute plea that he understand and trust her.

'What's troubling you, Mrs. Packwood?' he said gently.

In spite of her obvious distress she was a handsome woman. He wondered what had induced her to marry a coarse, brutal man like Packwood. It could hardly have been money, for the man hadn't always been prosperous and powerful. He was once another small operator on the far side of the Hueco Hills.

'My conscience,' she said. 'I know they're trying to frame you for killing Tarrone. I also know how he died, and that was bad enough. I brought you something. Here.' She reached in the pocket of her skirt and brought out a

49

trinket which she extended. 'I think that belongs to Luke Gallatin.'

'Why, yes,' Pick said, turning the piece over in his hand. It was a weatherproof match case of hammered silver. The initials LG were engraved on one side. Luke didn't carry it often, for fear of losing it. But Pick had seen it and knew it to be a present from his wife. 'Where did you get it, Mrs. Packwood?'

'One of my husband's men stole it from Big Springs,' she said in a dull voice. 'You must believe that he doesn't confide in me. My first intimation of what's going on was when you stopped us on the road about Tarrone. I knew from what I saw happening afterward that you were right. I know Wells has wanted that water hole for a long while. So I've been watching things. There was considerable agitation at Clover Leaf yesterday. A man brought word that Gallatin knew you weren't riding your starface at the time Tarrone was killed, that it had been stolen previously.'

'But this match case—'

'I'm coming to that. If you've been at Clover Leaf you know Wells's office is on one end of the main house. Frankly, I eavesdropped. Wells told a man to get something from Big Springs that was clearly the property of Luke Gallatin. Later the man came back with that trinket. He apparently had a chance to search the house.'

Pick nodded. 'Luke was over here. Old

50

Mike probably was up on the range.'

She looked at him again, beseechingly, overwrought. 'I heard them discuss a way to discredit what Gallatin and Terry would say to support you. That was to make them appear to be the riders with you that night. Not your own men, as they previously intended. They meant to plant the match case somewhere around Josh Springs, as if Luke had dropped it unknowingly. It might look fishy, yet it would tend to impeach him as a witness in your defense, too.'

'It would get him discounted,' Pick said dryly. 'The sheriff was to find it, I suppose.'

'Or the Tarrones. I couldn't let them frame three innocent people. He put the match case in his desk until later, and I stole it. I wouldn't want to betray my own husband to the law, Mr. Atherton. But I can stop him from compounding his guilt. Do you understand?'

'I do, and I'm obliged.'

She seemed relieved. 'Thank you. I thought at first I would only throw the case away. Then I realized you ought to know that they're attempting to implicate the Big Springs men, too. I thought I had better show you the trinket to convince you it isn't a trick.'

'Are you going to be suspected of this?'

'I don't think so. My husband underestimates my intelligence.' Abby Packwood smiled wearily. 'It's strange that I did this, that I want you to think well of me.

51

He hates you in a frightening way. He's never forgiven you for buying Mesa when he thought he had it in his grip.'

'To be frank, I always wondered why you married him.'

She nodded. 'I met him on the Coast. He can be so much the gentleman when he wants. I'd lived with him a while before I discovered what a foment of emotion he is. He knew when I married him that I didn't love him, only an illusion I mistook for him. He watched me become disillusioned day by day. The vicious streak he has made him hurry it along, destroying the last of my respect for him. And for myself, I guess, for having been so utterly naïve.'

She rose, tall and slender, and moved restlessly to the steps. A moment later she was mounted and gone.

It hadn't occurred to him to distrust her. What she had done was too sincere. He could appreciate the struggle she had gone through in reaching the decision to array herself against the man the vows of marriage bound her to so inescapably. He knew what her predicament would be if Packwood learned what she had done, which he very well might.

In consequence Packwood was in for a surprise when he was ready to plant the evidence intended to discredit the Big Springs men. At the moment he was tied up with the sheriff, prevented from saying too much by his reliance on his stratagem. He had men at Josh Springs and others passing back and forth. It would have been easy to drop the case somewhere and later see that Sunderleaf learned of it. And, relying on that until he learned of his folly, Packwood would be prevented from taking other steps.

CHAPTER FIVE

When the Santa Fe passenger snaked out of Cajon Pass and lined on the Mojave, Olive Gallatin had a moment of panic. The desert in all its pushing heat, dust, and dryness swept away on both sides of the track until it seemed to fill the world. Craning backward, she saw the coast mountains and their green slopes. Instead of steadying her nerves the sight only increased the riot in them. She just couldn't return to Big Springs Ranch. She would get off at Victorville and take the next train back to San Bernardino, where she should have stayed.

'Peanuts—candy—papers—playing cards—souvenirs—'

The train butcher came through the car, making his flat-voiced pitch. She watched his thin back as he lurched up the aisle and out the forward door. She thought the sway of the car would upset her stomach. What would she do if she were sick in that awful, helpless way that had happened so often lately? They said she would be over that phase in a few weeks, which did her no good now.

She was in the first coach back from the smoker and sat with a stiff, aching back on the edge of the dusty green seat. The rail breaks sent up the ticking of a runaway clock. The coach swayed even worse as the train picked up speed on the straightaway. Again the sickness gathered, more pronounced and overwhelming. Her tensed legs pushed at the floor.

All the other seats held people, some women in neat traveling oufits like her own and a few men in business suits. But most of the others were desert folk, miners and miners' families going out to Calico or Greenwater or Rhyolite. They all looked stolid in the stifling heat, and she hoped that she did, too, and not frightened. It was bad enough knowing secretly what a coward she was. She looked straight forward now, not at the buff and gray desolation of the Mojave. She wondered if she could stand it until she was back with her parents where she belonged.

The track kept curving and the car kept swaying and a lump had gathered tightly in her stomach. She noticed the woman across the way staring at her curiously. She had a small boy in overalls with her and maybe she guessed what was wrong. Olive swallowed hard. No one could guess how impossible it was for her to go back to the Amargosa, why she must get off this pitching thing at Victorville and return to the place where she had been happy for two short weeks. Victorville was the first desert town, by the river and among the trees.

It wouldn't take long to reach there, maybe half an hour, if only she could keep everything from coming up that long. She glanced up to see how easily she could get down her one bag. No one had piled anything on it. She would get it casually, as if this had been her destination all along. If she encountered the conductor at the steps she would tell him—well, something that would make him take it for granted.

Her spine stiffened when she heard the high running scream of the whistle. Glancing through the dusty window opposite, she saw from a thin line of cottonwoods that they were angling toward the river. The Mojave—the same name as the desert, the one running stream in all that simmering solitude worth a place on the map.

The woman across caught her eye, leaned forward, and said, 'It's hotter even than when I went out. It's so nice on the Coast. Once we even had rain.' There was wistfulness in her voice and beads of sweat on her upper lip. The little boy fidgeted and put all four fingers in his mouth. The woman pulled them out and spatted the hand.

Olive managed to smile. 'I know. It was wonderful.'

She leaned back, thinking about that downpour, how when she felt it in the atmosphere she hurried outdoors. The sky at the moment had been a mixture of bright sun and dark clouds. Then the rain curtain swept over everything with its soft warm gray, its glorious feel of Godgiven moisture brought by the clouds from the sea. In a moment the rain pelted her and the mountains behind the city. It soaked her and satisfied a craving so long denied it was like a lover possessing her.

The little boy across had stood up on the seat and was watching out the window. Olive wondered about the father. Only a man could make a woman undergo this journey into perdition time and again. Once she had been able to do it, too. But she had been a bride then, so very much in love with Luke she would have set up housekeeping in Death Valley itself had that been necessary. She was still in love—No, perhaps that was wrong. Being in love and simply loving a man were not alike. Being in love was romance and illusion. Loving was reality, a good part heartbreak and resentment and yet captivity, too, because one loved inseparably.

They simply hadn't got along, she and Luke. Living with him on the Amargosa had been very different from seeing him on evenings and weekends in Rhyolite, where she had been teaching school when they met. That had been winter. She had not yet undergone a summer when there wasn't a feel of rain in the air for months. She would go back to her parents' house and write him of their coming child, the surprise she had gotten on her visit home. She would tell him she could neither bear nor rear it on the desert, that he simply had to find work on the Coast. She would remind him how the Piutes said no one had any business on the desert who could not live in the shade of an arrow. Well, she couldn't and she belonged elsewhere.

The conductor came into the car and called, 'Victorville!' three times before he went out the other end, the door slamming behind him. The train drew closer to the river. People began to stir, and she realized with relief that others would get off. She stood up and got down her grip, steadying herself by the seat back. The train hadn't slowed yet, so she sat down again. She realized that her stomach was settled now, her trembling over.

Its bell clanging, the train ran into the hot desert town. Olive went down the aisle with people pushing behind her. She swayed when the train squalled to a stop, went forward, and found the brakeman guarding the steps.

As the train stopped he dropped off, and she followed. People were waiting to get on, more hardened denizens of the Mojave going farther into its wastes. She passed them and hurried toward the depot and the door to its waiting room.

At the door she stopped with the strange feeling one had when he knew he had forgotten something and couldn't quite recall it. Then it came to mind, the last thing Luke had said before she left him at Long String, 'Have a good time, honey, but it's gonna be lonesome without you—'

Hesitantly, she took her hand off the doorknob and stood lost in thought. Behind her someone cried, 'Board!' in a drawn-out way and, whirling, she ran back to the car steps. She hesitated for only a breath before she climbed them.

A man had taken her seat, and all the others were now filled. The little boy was occupying half a seat, his fingers in his mouth again, but his mother was staring out the window. Olive noticed that the man in her former seat was young and well dressed. He looked up when he grew aware of her and took his inventory of her. Touching his hat, he slid to the aisle side and stood up.

'If you don't mind sharing a seat, ma'am.'

He thought she had just got on, did not realize he had displaced her. Her brief glance showed that his eyes were lively and a little prowling, but he seemed well bred.

'Thank you.'

She let him lift her grip to the rack and sat down, moving over to the window and fixing her attention on the dusty wagon road between the car tracks and the town's few sun-baked buildings. The train started with a lurch and was soon running again on the desert, following the Mojave Wash into the heart of it. She felt calm, settled, ashamed of the weakness that had made her do what she did back there.

The man said, 'Maybe I could get the

window open.'

'Thank you, but that only makes it hotter and dustier.'

'Oh. I've never been out this way before.'

She was supposed to ask him why he was out here now and where he was going or permit him to volunteer it, but she didn't and he accepted the gentle rebuff. A little later he got up and moved forward toward the smoking car. She leaned back in the seat and closed her eyes.

She'd be like the woman across the aisle in a few years, as stolidly resigned, as weather-stained, perhaps as heavy. The slimness was going to leave her body in the next months and maybe, without the right care, it would never come back. The vitality would fade from her hair, and something would happen to the eyes she knew to be her best feature. She wondered how much this woman still loved her husband. It could be she hated him.

Olive ate lunch in a Harvey house and made the change to the Tidewater at Ludlow Station, deep in the desert. Only a part of the people in her car changed with her, the woman and the little boy going on toward Needles. The man had not come back from the smoking car, nor did she see him at the changeover. The second train panted its way through the ancient dry lakes and worn-down ranges, and thus in the early dusk she stepped down to the cinders at Long String.

Luke was not there waiting; she couldn't see him anywhere.

It gave her the worst feeling of her life, not barring her panic on the far side of the desert. The whole Amargosa seemed to rush in upon her. The fear struck through her that something had happened to him. There had been trouble again with Clover Leaf, the fear that had wormed in her mind since their marriage, that had done so much to make her hate the country.

Four people waited for her to move away from the car steps. A haggard woman placed her hand on the shoulder of an impatient boy of about sixteen who wanted to duck round and go up into the coach. A young woman stood in fixed patience, something in her eyes making its impact on Olive. Behind her was a man Olive recognized, a man Luke hated intensely, Pierce Hannegan, who was the foreman at Clover Leaf.

Hannegan's eyes were mocking as they regarded her, but he failed to speak. Then, still hunting Luke desperately with her eyes, she looked forward along the train and saw it. They were loading a long box off an express truck into the side door of the baggage car. She knew it contained a body.

'Who—is it?' she said involuntarily to Hannegan.

He didn't answer, and the others didn't seem to hear. Olive moved aside, not daring to

61

look forward again, while the others made their stolid way up the car steps. She was still standing there numbly when the train moved on.

A man walked toward the end of the depot with a mail sack slung over his shoulder. Another was drawing on the tongue of the express truck. She hurried toward him, a man whom she had noticed here before but who had no idea who she was.

'Was somebody killed?' she said.

The man didn't look at her and kept the truck trundling toward the door of the express office while he answered. 'I'll say there was. Another water-hole killing.'

'Where?'

'Over in Hueco Basin.'

She thought she would faint. 'Do you know who it was?' she said insistently.

The depot man shook his head. 'Only that it was some squatter again, the usual case. That was his family got on the train with Hannegan. Must be friends of his. Anyhow, he bought their tickets.'

Her relief was immense and very short-lived. Something had gone on in her absence that Luke had not written about. That meant he was involved, too, or he would have been here. She ran down beside the sunblistered depot to the street where it came off the desert. In another half hour it would be wholly dark, for there was little twilight in this country, and she had to get to Big Springs somehow.

The liveryman was stubborn. 'Ma'am, I can't rent you a rig to strike across the desert by yourself at night. And I've got nobody to drive you.'

'I'll pay any amount you ask.'

'That ain't the point. I don't have anybody on tap.'

'You drive me—please.'

'Sorry, ma'am. It's out of the question.'

She turned away, desperate enough to strike out on foot. She moved blindly toward the depot. Luke knew when she was coming back, had confirmed the date in a letter. Then, when she reached the tracks, she saw well out on the desert some kind of vehicle drawing toward Long String through the thickening darkness. She waited there, her knees weak and trembling.

It was Luke, who drove swiftly into town and jumped down over the wheel. She saw at a glance that he was all right and she was instantly, intensely angry.

She beat his chest with her fists when he put his arms about her. 'Why weren't you here?' she said furiously.

'I couldn't help it and I'll tell you all about it. Now—now—' But she wasn't going to cry, she was too shakingly hostile. 'We'll get something to eat,' he said gently, 'and start right back.'

'I'm not hungry.'

'Then I'll get something to eat on the way.'

He helped her up to the seat, put in her grip, then drove down to the store. She said nothing more, waiting stolidly while he went in and returned with a wedge of cheese and a sack of crackers. Then they headed out of town into the eternal heat of the desert. She felt its rough sucking dryness on her face and she was shocked at how much she had grown to fear and hate it.

Finally she faced up, saying, 'Who was killed?'

Luke turned his head to look at her. He let out a long breath. 'So that's what scared you. The sheriff said Hannegan was taking the body and family to Rhyolite.'

'Who are they and what happened?' she said insistently.

Luke slung his head to the side and sighed. 'Well, there's trouble. Packwood's on the move again. He spotted a man at Josh Springs, and somebody shot up the place and killed the squatter. They're trying to job Pick Atherton and the Mesa boys. That's why I was late. I had to wait for the sheriff and got a later start for town than I intended. I'm sorry, but I wasn't very late, and there's no cause for you to be so upset.'

'Why did you have to see the sheriff?' she said, unplacated.

'The only thing standing between Pick and

the gallows is me and Mike. Clover Leaf left a dead Mesa horse at Josh Springs after the killing. Me and Mike know it was stolen beforehand. Pick had been over to tell and warn us. That's something Packwood never figured on, and it might upset his wagon.'

Her chest was tight. 'That'll draw you into the trouble with them.'

'God Almighty, Olive,' he said explosively. 'Don't you realize I've been in trouble ever since Clover Leaf started to take over the basin?'

'But you promised—'

'And if you were half a woman you'd never have made me.'

That was like a giant hammer hitting her on top of the head. She closed her eyes. Her voice failed, her breath nearly stopped. Coldness streamed through her body, and she wished she could die. She couldn't, and the numbness began to thaw, the rage gone, the fear replacing it. She had always known his secret bitterness, his yearning to take back his own. She knew that his rebellion now was full and final.

The buckboard ran on, and she sat thinking of how she had expected it to be when she came home. The reunion should have wiped out all the obstacles and all the tensions, their denied bodies aflame in a night so like a wedding night. In the sweet aftermath of that she had intended to tell him about their child.

65

Now she could not, for it would seem to him to be another fetter.

After a while his quieter voice said, 'I wish you'd try to understand, Olive.'

'I do, but it's so frightening.'

'How was San Berdue?' That was what all the habitues called San Bernardino. He was relaxing.

'All right, but I didn't feel very good—' She caught herself. 'Change of climate, I guess. Did you finish the calf branding?'

He nodded. 'The stuff's in the mountains. So little of it we can work it from home where we used to camp up there all summer. Don't you see?'

She didn't want his mind to return to the trouble, for she didn't want her own to do it. 'How's Mike?' She knew Luke thought a lot of the old puncher who had worked for his father so long.

'Grouchy as ever.'

'I wish he liked me.'

'He don't dislike you, Olive. Mike's just shy of women.'

'My kind, anyway.'

'Why'd you say that?'

She tried to laugh. 'I don't resent it, because he's right. I'm not a good ranch wife. I'm not like the women who fought off Indians with one hand while nursing a baby—' She caught herself again.

'There's no longer a need for that kind of

women.'

'You don't think so?' she said.

The buckboard traveled steadily, the tired horses alternating between a walk and slow trot. Luke didn't try to hurry them. He had the patience of a Piute in some things, while being as restless as she was in others. The burning stars came out, and presently the desert was fully about them, although in pale relief. She listened to the soft clop of the horses' hoofs on the sand. Once, not far away, a coyote cry went racketing across the night. Long later she saw foothills rise on the forward horizon. They were bare and scorched but better than the desert.

CHAPTER SIX

Reining in his horse beside Tony Revella's where the trail struck into the Sapphires, Pick glanced keenly at the man. Revella was from the South Pahrump and had ridden through on his way to the railroad. Although the sheriff had left the basin without an arrest, the tensions were still high in Pick. He knew it might only be a matter of time. Sunderleaf wasn't sure yet, that was all.

He said, 'You'll find it easy to reach our herd, Tony. The boys can set you on the right trail to the desert. Ask Blackie to do that, and tell Pecos I want him to come down here.' Being old acquaintances, he had explained matters to Revella, who was not familiar with this end of the country. He had asked him to do a favor, since he was going outside.

Revella was a tall, lean man with a Latin's grace and courtesy. 'Sure three new men's all you'll need?' he said.

'If they come from Bird Quigley in Vegas. Just tell him I want fighting men at fighting pay.'

'I'll wire him as soon as I hit the railroad,' Revella said. 'Good luck.' They shook hands, and Revella rode on up the slope of the mountain.

Pick turned west. The day was another hot

one, bursting out of a dazzling dawn. A blistering breeze stirred up the slope and dried his perspiration as fast as he leaked it. On his left the great basin floor ran under heat waves like molten mica. The rose and blue haze of the desert rubbed out the far sky.

He clung to the higher slope until he was behind Josh Springs, then swung down toward the watering, keeping himself well covered. Just back from the rim above the Joshua patch he dismounted and left his horse, moving on afoot. Presently he looked down at the watering and its adobe hut and barbed-wire enclosure. The Tarrone wagon still stood where it had been parked initially. The two ribby horses still grazed in the company of a couple wearing the Clover Leaf iron. The punchers Hannegan had left to hold the springs were indoors, probably killing time with a deck of cards.

He found a notch in the inconsequential rim and dropped down among the Joshuas, stepping carefully and continuing on at once. The back of the structure below presented him with a solid block wall of dusty tan. He moved down to it without creating an alarm. There he halted arid drew in several quiet breaths, bringing up his gun. Then, ducked over, he slid along the left-hand wall and presented himself in the doorway, the gun gripped in his hand.

'All right, boys,' he said quietly. 'You're relieved. Mesa still owns this water and will do the guarding it needs.'

They stared at the gun that covered them, Sandy Tolliver and Leek Hollis. Their astonishment flattened the features of their weathered faces. Tolliver's leg muscles lifted him slightly, but a warning from Pick relaxed them. They both sat at the table, still holding card hands, caught flat-footed and furious about it. For an instant Pick thought they would try to shoot it out. Being two of Hannegan's select hands, they stood a chance in combination.

'Don't crowd your luck,' Pick said, his voice still quiet.

The yellow-haired Tolliver was the wild one of the pair, while Leek Hollis was several years older. Hollis grunted, 'Take it easy, Sandy,' and returned his hostile eyes to Pick. 'You're making a mistake, Atherton. You can't get away with it.'

'On your feet.'

He told them to drop their shell belts, ready to shoot them if they crowded him. Hollis obeyed, but Tolliver's hands lingered over the belt buckle. Then his belt dropped also. At Pick's snapped words they edged around him and moved outdoors. He kicked the weapons into a back corner and followed out.

He made them carry their rigs to their horses and saddle them where they stood. 'Now, get off Mesa,' he said flatly, 'and take this message to Packwood. Any Clover Leaf

70

man caught on our range without good reason will be killed on sight. That means what we regard as our range, not what he does.'

They stepped across their horses. Hollis said in a dull, furious way, 'That's a tall order, Atherton.'

'Test it if you feel lucky.'

'We feel lucky.'

He swung his horse and left in a burst of speed, Tolliver following. They slanted southwest toward Reedy Smith's line fence. Pick watched them steadily until they had started to fade in the dust they left behind.

He brought down his own horse, then rolled a cigarette. Considerable of the Tarrones' camp gear was still scattered about. He carried it to the wagon and loaded it, afterward bringing in their horses and harnessing them to the wagon. Tying his own horse behind, he mounted to the seat and drove out toward Wagon Tire Well.

Sam Masterson watched him pull in under the cottonwoods in marked surprise. 'What the hell're you doing with that fleabitten outfit?' he called.

Pick stopped the wagon and jumped down. 'Nothing you don't want me to, Sam,' he said. 'But I'd like to park it here for them to pick up when they get back from Rhyolite.'

'What about them Clover Leaf hands?'

'They got discouraged with it for the moment. I made my stand, Sam, and I've got to get this outfit off Mesa and keep it off.'

'Then take it over to Smith or Finney. They're Packwood stooges, and he brought them drifters here. Why dump them on me?' Sam was sympathetic, but he also liked his privacy as he had proved for thirty years.

'Because I'm sorry for them, Sam, and so are you. That shiftless cuss is dead, but we can't take it for granted the others are of the same stripe.'

'I don't think they are,' Sam said.

'So let's deal them out of what's bound to be a nasty fight. You've been on this water too long for Packwood to dispute your rights here. He's professed sympathy for the Tarrones. So he can't make anything out of you sheltering them till they're ready to travel on.'

'What if they don't want to travel on?' Sam said. 'That girl's stubborn.'

'I don't think they'd take advantage of a man who tried to be good to them, Sam. Do you?'

'Guess I don't. All right, leave the rig here and let's see what comes of it.'

Pick unhitched the scrubby team, watered and put it back on picket. Stepping across his own horse, he rode back to Josh Springs.

Bloated and growing odorous, the dead horse still lay down the strands of barbed wire from the adobe. Pick observed that the saddle had been worked off and taken away, possibly by Sunderleaf in hope of tracing its ownership.

Pick wanted to dispose of the carcass, no small job. Then it occurred to him that its reeking unpleasantness would soon be strong enough to offset any idea Piper might have about coming back here.

That would not apply to Packwood, who wouldn't release his grip on the watering without a struggle. Pick dismissed the idea of putting his own man here. It was better to keep them all free to move about as needed. With the Tarrones no longer at Josh to sustain his thin excuse of protecting them, Packwood would have to move openly the next time. It might not be where expected.

Going to the adobe, Pick got the gun rigs he had forced Hollis and Tolliver to shuck off and took them out with him. Mounting, he headed across the flat, this time bearing toward Reedy Smith's line fence between the Drys and the playa. He hung the weapons on the Texas gate when he reached the fence. He swung east toward Eagle Point and its gap to the mesa's far side.

The morning had gone, and he fixed a meal at headquarters. Pecos rode in just as he was ready to eat, and they sat down together. Apparently Revella hadn't lingered to explain much, for Pecos was curious.

'Here I am and hoping it's for a real nasty purpose.'

'The springs have been vacated,' Pick said, 'and I aim to keep it that way. Revella's ordering me some more men out of Vegas. When they get here a couple will take over the herd. Then I can have you and Blackie and the best one of them with me. The intention ought to suit you. We'll get back what Plez Brown and Charlie Gallatin lost to Clover Leaf.'

Pecos said nothing, but his eyes gleamed.

That afternoon they brought in the loose horses and started shoeing them to equip the enlarged outfit with a mount. Pick knew he would have to send to Long String for more chuck and ammunition. When they had eaten supper he rode out toward Big Springs to see Luke Gallatin, for whom he felt an increased respect and a great deal of gratitude.

Only Mike Terry was on hand, a lean, dour man close to seventy who with Sam was a pioneer in the Hueco. 'Why, Luke and the missus went for a ride after supper,' he said. 'Up to the summer range. Might run into them if you want to head up that way.'

'No rush.' Pick knew Olive had only been home a day, that they would rather be by themselves. 'Just tell Luke I run Packwood's punchers off Josh Springs and warned them to keep off our range. They might try for another surprise.'

'We're on the lookout,' Mike said. 'Luke kicked over the traces, finally. He made it plain to—well, he made it plain that we've got to fight or go under.'

'I know what he's up against.'

74

'City women,' Mike said with a snort. 'They think things have got to be done polite. Maybe that works in a town but not around here. She still don't like the deal. They've rowed ever since she got back. Private like, but a man can tell from the way they act toward each other.'

'She's a good woman, Mike.'

'Goodness don't win pots in this country.'

Pick agreed but didn't share Mike's impatience with Olive. San Bernardino, where she grew up, was a fairsized city that took law and order for granted. It had civilized comforts, a better climate, more pleasant surroundings. A woman couldn't find a sharper contrast than between it and this desert country, where the nearest neighbors were eight miles off and all men. It was a pity things had been so she and Abby Packwood couldn't get acquainted.

Pecos had shaken down when Pick reached Mesa, and Pick turned in. They were both up with the morning star and put in the forenoon on routine work. After the midday meal they headed for Wagon Tire Well. Pierce Hannegan should be back sometime that afternoon with the little party he had escorted to Rhyolite with such false gallantry. Pick didn't want Sam to bear the brunt of Hannegan's wrath and had no idea how the Tarrones would take the enforced change. They reached Sam's in the first heat of the afternoon.

It was about two o'clock when Hannegan's

75

buckboard wheeled in from the direction of Josh Springs, whence he had followed the tracks of the Tarrone wagon. The women were in the seat with him, and a teenage boy dangled his legs out the back end. Hannegan's face was twisted as he stopped, his gaze riveted on Pick.

'So you're still up to your dirty work,' he said in a heavy voice.

'Cut out the acting, Hannegan,' Pick said quietly. 'Sam's inviting the Tarrones to camp here. There's as much water and more shade. He guarantees to protect them even better than you would. By which I mean, without a hidden motive.'

Hannegan bristled, thought better of it, and subsided. Sam touched his droopy hat to the older woman. 'You can use my shack, ma'am. Ain't got much of a selection in grub, but there's plenty such as it is. It'd be a pleasure to eat a woman's cooking. Don't recall when I last did.'

The appeal was so sincere it reached her, and she seemed drawn by the comfort of Wagon Tire in contrast to the desolation and painful memories at Josh Springs.

Hannegan noted her weakening. His eyes glinted. Piper sat in stony hostility but must have been woman enough to appreciate Sam's offer. The old man had come to them in their trouble, trying to help. She must remember that, whatever she thought of Pick Atherton.

76

'Don't let them trick you,' Hannegan said waspishly. 'The old coot might be harmless, but you've seen a sample of Atherton. Let him lure you off the springs and you'll surrender the rights you established.'

'We're not surrendering a darned thing,' Piper said hotly. 'But we're so beat I reckon we'll stay here one night.' Her stare fixed on Pick. 'You understand that? We aren't quitting Josh Springs. You moved us, we didn't, and we aim to go back.'

'You're going back right now,' Hannegan said roughly. His bitter glare seemed to shock her a little. He swung to look at the old wagon. 'Get the horses, Rip. We'll get them hitched.'

Mrs. Tarrone intervened. 'I reckon we'll light here, Mr. Hannegan. You've been obliging, but we aim to make up our own minds about things.' She had more spirit than Pick had expected. She turned on the seat to meet the blunt stare of Hannegan's eyes. She wasn't afraid of him. As he helped her down, Pick realized the extent of her exhaustion, for she sagged heavily against him.

'You all right, Ma?' Piper said anxiously, springing to the ground.

'I'm tuckered out.'

That seemed to settle it with Piper. She turned to call to the truculent-faced boy standing behind the buckboard.

'Come help, Rip.'

The three of them moved toward the shack.

Regarding Hannegan coolly, Pick said, 'If you don't get started for Clover Leaf, Hannegan, you're going to be late for your dinner.'

Hannegan drove away in a rush. Knowing how unwelcome they were now, Pick and Pecos struck out for Mesa.

CHAPTER SEVEN

Hannegan turned into a gap where a wedging plain split into the Hueco Hills. Afterward he followed a wash toward the point where Clover Leaf headquarters lay stained against the buff of the hills. Old cottonwoods threw their shade across the wheeled-out road he followed on a gradual bend to the south. It was a welcome change after the heat of the Amargosa, which he had crossed that forenoon in mounting impatience with his charges.

A graying, hard-set man with years of desert life and work behind him, Hannegan was used to command. He had been Packwood's foreman for several years. He had expected to manipulate the Tarrones like puppets in return for his help. Though politely appreciative they had all proved independent, even the fuzz-cheeked boy.

Hannegan put the Tarrones aside momentarily and directed his attention ahead. These headquarters were of late vintage, the old layout having been beyond the belt of hills. In preparation for his marriage and expansion he hoped to make of the ranch, Packwood had chosen to build on this side. The setting was more to a woman's taste, more central to future operations, and closer to the railroad.

As he drew closer, Hannegan slid an appreciative eye over the corrals and stables. Finally he looked at the long house of stone and timber that was probably the most lavish ranch house in the south end of Nevada. He wheeled into the yard, yelled for old Mack, the roustabout, and told him to take care of the tired team.

Packwood's office was on the end of a wing of the house. It had an outside door so the help could come and go without contact with the house proper. The fact that Hannegan had himself sprung from a grubby, hardbitten line made him resentful of this segregation of classes. Yet there was compensation in his secret opinion. Packwood chose mainly, he believed, to keep his restless wife out of the eye of the younger men on the spread. Some of them respected no one's property.

For several days he had wondered how Packwood would react if he knew his wife had visited Pick Atherton secretly at Mesa headquarters. Hannegan had caught onto it entirely by accident while riding to the ranch from Josh Springs. He had seen her on the high mesa, himself unobserved, a most unusual place for her to be. Spying from the rim, he had watched her approach the house, where she had remained for several minutes.

It had puzzled him deeply, and he wasn't yet ready to tell her husband that she was trafficking with the enemy. Packwood would be apt to kill her. Hannegan had no sympathy for her. But if she was to be tormented, he wouldn't mind applying a little of it on his own hook. She had always been hoity-toity with him, thus constituting a challenge.

His boot heels hit the flagging outside the office. His knuckles made a tattoo on the door, then he opened it and stepped in. Packwood had his feet on the desk while he perused a stockman's journal, which he tossed aside when he looked up at his big foreman.

'How'd it go?' he said without other greeting, although Hannegan had been away several days.

This persistent lack of respect had bred in Hannegan an offsetting contrariness. He cuffed back his dusty hat and without answering sauntered to a sagging leather chair under the window. Seated, he shook his head and answered enigmatically, solely to irritate as he was irritated.

'Good and bad, I reckon.'

Packwood waited, scowling. Hannegan knew he had banked heavily on raking in the whole pot in what had seemed a devilishly clever strike at Mesa. The men must have come in from Josh Springs to give him an inkling that this wasn't going to happen immediately. Hannegan refused to elaborate.

'Well?' Packwood said.

Having scored his minor triumph, Hannegan relented. 'There's plenty of hard

81

feeling against Atherton over the killing of Tarrone. Nobody likes to see women shot up, even squatter women. The inquest was no more than what we knew it would be, a formality. From here on it's the sheriff and district attorney and the grand jury if we can work it. How'd you get along with the sheriff?' He was waiting to hear what had happened to the men at Josh Springs to find out how Atherton could have pulled the stunt he did.

'Sunderleaf's cautious,' Packwood said. 'He seen Luke Gallatin before he come here, so he knew their side about that starface. I didn't even hint that Gallatin and Terry could be in it with Atherton. That match case will do that better. By the way, did you take it?'

'Take it? You said if it was found too soon it would look pat.'

Packwood's brow pulled into a frown. He drew open the middle desk drawer and went through it carefully. He did the same with the other drawers, his scowl darkening steadily. Finally he quit and rubbed his jaw.

'My God,' he said. 'Somebody must have stole the thing.'

A sudden, persuading suspicion crawled into Hannegan's mind. Had Abby guessed, and even then would she dare to do a thing like that? It was possible. She was the high-toned one, full of pride and righteousness. She had been to Mesa in secret. But he wasn't going to tell Packwood what he thought, at least not yet.

'Who'd have stole it?' Hannegan said. 'Who knew about it but you and me? And Fred Gillege, who got it from Big Springs for us.'

Packwood shook his head, bewildered and worried.

'It'd most likely be somebody from Mesa or Big Springs. Somebody who saw Gillege poking around over there. Damn it, Pierce, I was banking everything on that play. Without it Atherton's got as good a case against us as we've got against him.'

'Ten to one he's got the match case now,' Hannegan said in a drawl. He didn't want Packwood to arrive at the truth yet, that was an advantage he meant to keep in his own hands as long as possible. He changed the subject. 'What happened at Josh Springs? Did you pull the boys off?'

Packwood shook his head bitterly. 'Atherton surprised and disarmed them and sent them in. Believe me, I took the hide off them. But I decided to wait till the Tarrones returned to put them back. We've got to keep ourselves looking good after that other upset. Now that they're there again, we've got an excuse for being there ourselves.'

'They're not there, though. Atherton moved their wagon to Wagon Tire. He and Masterson persuaded them to put up there. Anyhow, for tonight.'

'They're going back to Josh,' Packwood said

83

angrily. 'We got a break in finding that girl's got so much spunk. We're going to make use of it.'

Hannegan shook his head. 'Maybe not. The older woman's got a backbone, too, and I don't think she trusts us an inch.'

Packwood's fingers drummed the desk, his frown deepening. For a moment he pursued some thought, unconsciously shaking his head. 'We've got to change their minds, Pierce. And we've got to find a new way to throw dust in Sunderleaf's eyes.'

'Not easy now.'

Nodding, Packwood said, 'Well, it took Luke a long time to stiffen his neck. The reason is an open secret. His wife. Maybe he won't scare out again, but I bet she would.'

'How?'

'Maybe I know how,' Packwood said with a glint in his eye. 'If something scared the hell out of her, he might tone down his story. He might be willing to change it in secret testimony to the grand jury.'

'There's still Mike Terry. He seen Atherton wasn't riding the starface that night. He knows it was stolen before the shoot-up.'

Packwood smiled coldly. 'Exactly. You're going to kill old Terry.'

Hannegan was a well-controlled man, but his eyes bulged. 'My God, Wells, not when we're already in a tight spot.'

'We've jumped off and we've got to keep

jumping. That's the only way to recover our ground. If lightning strikes that close to home Olive Gallatin will go to pieces. Luke might even be willing to accept our offer for the ranch. That would leave us free to concentrate on Mesa.'

Hannegan had long been aware of the recklessness in his employer, which seemed to spring from some simmering cavern of concealed emotion. Packwood didn't mean an apparent murder, of course. They would find a way to do it that would minimize the danger to Clover Leaf while getting the message to the Gallatins. That was easy in this wild country, so often crisscrossed by floating hoodlums from the mining camps and outlaws from all points of the West. The idea began to appeal to the brash side of Hannegan himself. He nodded appreciatively.

'We'd have a far better springboard from Big Springs than from Josh. So it wouldn't matter what the Tarrones do or think.'

'You're getting the idea, and it's worth the risk.'

'By God, you're right,' Hannegan said. 'Terry's a tough old turkey, though, and a damned good shot. I've seen him unlimber.'

'You're supposed to be smarter, at least. Prove it.'

Hannegan rubbed his jaw. 'Maybe I will.' He rose, much of the tiredness washed out of him by the excitement, his depression over the setbacks turned into a bright elation. 'How soon?'

'That's up to you and the chance you get. But the sooner the better.' Packwood fell silent. His wife had walked past the window, coming in from the ride she took each day. Hannegan felt a wicked delight, reminded of what he knew about her recent activity on such a ride. What if Packwood got the idea she was interested in Atherton as a man? And maybe she was, which had caused her to take that action. His knowledge itched on his tongue, but he knew there would be a time when it would be more useful to him. Nodding, he stepped out into the bright sunlight.

He washed up at the bunkhouse, then had the cook dish him some chuck left over from noon. Afterward he saddled a horse, ruminating on what had come to seem a very shrewd change in tactics. It was the way Packwood's mind worked. Step by step those bold slashes had brought the outfit up through the hills.

The most valuable range of all lay due ahead in the reaching meadowland held by Mesa and Big Springs. While he did not fully share Packwood's hatred of Atherton, the great ranch that would result appealed strongly to Hannegan. As its ramrod he would be in a position of enormous power himself. He was coming into that already.

He stepped across the horse and rode out.

There was a lot of range and work under his supervision. There were still men and cattle at the old ranch, and a new herd had been sifted through the hills between. All that kept him glued to the leather.

But he had a little prowling to do, and this had taken hold in him. He struck along the broadening flat. In about an hour his course brought him up at the fence separating this section from the Big Spring bench grass. There he idled while he rolled a cigarette, foreseeing the day when the long line fence could be torn out.

Presently he turned to the right, passing the fine watering already wrested from Big Springs. He poked on into a canyon leading to the grassy plateaus of the Piutes. Gallatin's main herd and dry bunch were up there, as were Gallatin and Terry during most of the daylight hours.

He topped out at a level where scrub oak appeared in black dots along the gentle slope, neighboring with nut pine and, on the upper rises, ragged stripes of yellow pine. The leathery skin of his face felt the stirring air, a little cooler here. He heard the air's faint murmur as it filtered through the higher timber. Sage lived at this level, its smell a pleasant change from the hot metal smell of the desert. He rode more cautiously, for he had come onto Big Springs' admitted range. His hard, keen eyes observed everything stirring about him.

He halted on a headland where roughs divided the plateau and let his horse get its wind. The day was so clear he could see across the desert to where snow peaks reared over the high Sierra. Lower ran the ranges that slashed the desert into its many blistered valleys, pooled in the heat and all but drowned in haze. The elemental violence stirred him.

He passed on through the roughs and instantly pulled up his horse. Not far below a rider sat facing the other way. He knew from the shapeless hat and slouched shoulders that it was Mike Terry. On a level, slightly beyond, a bunch of whitefaces grazed peacefully. The old cowhand was watching them.

Excitement rammed through Hannegan, and he pulled the carbine up from its boot, his eyes gleaming. For a moment he held the sights squarely on Terry's back, strongly tempted. It could be called the work of rustlers. Yet in the next breath he realized that, under the circumstances, there would have to be a better blind than that. He jammed the weapon back in the boot, quietly turned his horse, and withdrew.

Barely back under cover, he got a second surprise. Out of the tail of his eye he saw something move higher on the plateau, still visible to him, just at the edge of the timber. He stood on the stirrups long enough to take a reckless, searching look that way and saw the rider coming downgrade. White cloth made it more plainly visible, and he realized this would be the upper garment of a woman. He melted on into the roughs, cursing himself for his headlong action in lining a gun on the old fellow. It had been a heedless yielding to lust which kept him from considering that someone else might be near.

A woman on this range would be Gallatin's wife, probably up here with the men for a holiday. If she had seen and recognized him and his action, the thing could get sticky when something did happen to old Terry. But probably she hadn't. He would have been harder to make out against the rocks and brush, standing still. Neither the horse nor his own clothes were colored conspicuously. Then he had an idea.

Instead of turning back toward Clover Leaf he crossed over the ridge. If he were trailed this would leave the impression that it had been some chance riffraff, wondering what he could get out of the old puncher's pockets, then changing his mind. It would take a lot of unplanned riding, but he could drop down into the pass trail to Piute Wells. He would go on until he could lose his tracks on the heavily traveled freight road between Rhyolite and Las Vegas.

The far slope made rougher riding. When he was well north of the occupied range, he came back over, thereafter keeping himself blended against the edge of the timber. He was wondering now about Luke Gallatin and where he had been when the crazy thing happened. He kept puzzling about himself. A man could be a study in contradictions, moving with near wizardry at times, again acting in utter stupidity.

He came down the south slope of the Piute pass well beyond Big Springs headquarters. There he turned east on a little-used trail out of the basin. He believed he had covered himself well now but would go on to make sure. Afterward he would cut back across the range and come out in the Hueco Hills. He relaxed in the saddle, observing that the afternoon was nearly gone.

He was a couple of miles beyond the pass when, coming out of a wash, he observed three riders on the road ahead. He had not seen them previously. That meant they had been resting in the black shade of the cuesta up there. Hannegan scowled, not liking to be seen this close to the pass. But they had already detected him, leaving him no choice. He rode on slackly, not showing his uneasiness. This subsided presently, for he recognized none of them. Obviously they were drifting punchers with their personals lashed to their saddles. They all wore guns.

They were hard-faced men who eyed him keenly, but they reined in, forcing him to do likewise. All showed trail grime and the red eyes of a long desert journey. One was tall, thin, but clearly the leader of the trio. He spoke for them.

'Howdy. This country's so all alike it's confusing. We on the trail to Hueco Basin?'

'That's right,' Hannegan said. 'But if you're hunting a town you should have stayed on the main road.'

'We're looking for Mesa Ranch. You know it?'

Hannegan narrowed his eyes. 'Sure. It's a damned small outfit if you want jobs.'

'They're hiring. Man in Vegas told us they're putting on guns. We brung guns.'

Hannegan had trouble concealing his surprise. It hadn't occurred to him, and probably not to Packwood, that Mesa would arm itself for an all-out fight. He said, 'I reckon somebody sent you on a wild-goose chase, friends. There's no trouble around here.'

'So?' the thin puncher said narrowly. 'Heard there was a water-hole killing. That sounds like trouble to me.'

'All right,' Hannegan admitted, 'but don't get on the wrong side of the fence. It was Mesa who done that killing.'

'Sounds like you're on the other side.'

'And so's the rest of this country. You're asking for trouble if you throw in with that outfit, boys.'

'We like trouble.'

Hannegan realized that he dared not admit his identity or he would have offered them jobs at more money, whatever Atherton had promised to pay. He was tempted anyway, but the thought of being accused of trying to shoot old Terry in the back was too chilling. He said, 'It's your business.'

'That's right, I reckon.'

The thin man nodded, and the three rode on.

Hannegan was surprised at the speed of his pulse. To that point he had thought only of Clover Leaf's chance at big winnings. Yet against sufficient force it could lose equally, for like all big ranches, it was itself vulnerable in many ways.

He realized it would have done no good to hire these men away from Mesa. If he was ready to throw everything into the fight Atherton would keep on hiring them. That led his thoughts back to Abby Packwood and her secret meeting with Atherton. His sense of Clover Leaf's blindness in a situation into which it had plunged heedlessly hit him hard. He rode on, carrying out the ruse forced upon him by his own folly.

CHAPTER EIGHT

The cattle in the sapphires were undisturbed, serenely grazing on the lush forest grass. Pick showed two of the new men the boundaries of Mesa's range, the water supply, then left them to handle the routine. Afterward, riding down from the resinous pines with Blackie Chase, he reflected on the men he had added to his payroll.

The evening before, when the three flint-eyed strangers arrived over the trail from Piute Wells, he had been taken aback by their appearance. But soap, water, and clean clothes had presented them in a better light. Now he was pretty sure he had what he wanted. The tall puncher, who gave the name of Hosea Sands, had been his choice for assignment to the home ranch and the moves he had in mind to make from there.

As they came down into the scattered oak and nut pine of the lower mountain, Blackie said, 'Sam got the Tarrones straightened out on what's what?'

'Well, they're not so bullheaded sure of things,' Pick said. 'I wish there was more to do for them. They're broke, and I don't know where they'll wind up if we make them move on.'

'Packwood was pretty generous with Mesa

real estate. Why not take a page from his book and set them up on land that he claims?'

Pick glanced at the puncher, who was joking. But an idea began to form in his mind. 'Maybe you hit something. Les Finney's setup at the Long String pass would be about right. That kid Rip is at the age where he could go two ways. Turn into a renegade or make a damned good cowhand. Between him and the girl, I think they'd make a go of running cattle.'

'Better have them there than Les Finney, anyway. But how'd you get Les to let go?'

'That's the louse in the bedroll,' Pick said.

For years, until bitten by the bug to set up for himself, Finney had ridden for Clover Leaf. There had never been any doubt why he had chosen to squat at Gap Springs back when Plez Brown had been unable to hold it. He was a tough nut like all the Clover Leaf outfit, but he must have a soft spot somewhere. Pick decided to look for it. That was one springs Mesa could let go to a friendly occupant, since the playa cut it off from the main ranch.

He had left Pecos and Hosea shoeing horses. The work was finished when he and. Blackie got back to the ranch. The morning was gone, and they ate their noon meal. During its course Pick outlined the procedure.

'Packwood succeeded in stirring up hard feelings against us,' he said, 'or our job would be simpler. Our first aim is to see Clover Leaf

94

don't grab off Josh again or make a pass at some other springs. Meanwhile I'd like to knock Finney and Smith off the range they grabbed in the old days. Finally, I'd sure like to move Packwood's fence back to the hills. We'd be as justified in all that as they were when they grabbed that range.'

Blackie nodded. 'Packwood's argument ought to work both ways.'

Pick smiled thinly. 'That's the idea. I'm glad to have you fellows to help me and I'm laying just one restriction on you. We only fight as dirty as they make us, but we fight harder than they do. Is that clear?'

His main question was about Sands, whose slat-thinness and oversized mouth gave him a half-comical look that was contradicted by a pair of steely gray eyes. Pick had asked them no questions. That had been a tacit agreement when he sent out for fighting men.

'I met a fellow on the trail yesterday,' Hosea said, 'who claimed your side already done what dirty work's been done in this squabble.'

'So?' Pick said. 'Who'd that be?'

'Dunno. Only said he was on the other side. Big man. Maybe forty, give or take.'

'Sounds like Hannegan,' Pecos said with interest. 'Where'd you meet him?'

'Other side of the pass. He was heading east.'

'Brand on his horse?'

Hosea's eyes glimmered. 'Kind of a cookie

95

cutter. It could be called a clover leaf.'

'Then it was Hannegan,' Pick said. 'I don't know what he was doing over there, but he's got cause to be partial.'

'I reckon,' Hosea said, and grinned.

Pick sent the others out to work the range. For his own part he struck north under the shading rim of the big mesa. He passed Eagle Point at an easy jog and in about an hour rode in to Wagon Tire Well. The Tarrone wagon was still parked under the cottonwoods. But he saw that the derelict family had accepted Sam's invitation to use his shack. Mrs. Tarrone looked out the door and said something over her shoulder. Piper appeared behind her, and this time she wasn't armed. Their reserved stares stayed on him as he swung down.

'Howdy,' Pick said, touching his hat. 'Sam off somewhere?'

'Saddled and went is all I know,' Mrs. Tarrone said.

'What do you want here, Atherton?' a heavier voice said behind Pick.

Turning, Pick saw Rip climb down from the old covered wagon. Following in his father's boot tracks, he apparently had been asleep there. He was overgrown and when he dropped to the ground he stood in a chip-on-shoulder attitude, his neck slung forward.

Pick gave him a nod. 'You're the one I wanted to see mainly. I need another hand if you're not scared of work.'

'What kind of work?'

'Depends on whether you can ride a horse.'

The appeal, good on most boys, was effective on Rip. His chin came up. 'You don't think we always lived on this wagon, do you? For a while my pa had a ranch. Me and Piper can ride as good as you can. And we aim to do it, running our own cattle.'

'When you've got them,' Pick said, 'and the necessary range. Meanwhile you've got to live. I could use a good rider your age, Rip. Wrangling, packing grub and salt to the summer camp, chores like that. Thirty a month and found.'

In spite of his lingering hostility, Rip was interested. But before he could speak his sister cut in.

'Wait a minute,' Piper said. 'What kind of a lowdown trick is it this time, Pick Atherton?' She came down the steps, looking rested now, a slender girl who was extra pretty when she wasn't holding a rifle on him.

'You know I didn't trick you, Piper,' Pick said quietly. 'Sam must have told you a dozen times what happened at Josh Springs.'

'He didn't see it. He only had your story about it. Maybe he chooses to believe it, but I don't.'

'You mean you won't own up you were wrong.'

Her eyes raked him, heavy with unforgiveness. 'It'll take some showing on your

97

part to prove I am,' she said with a toss of the head.

Dismissing the useless argument, Pick said, 'How about it, Rip?'

'You listen to me, Piper,' Mrs. Tarrone said tartly. 'We can't stay and mooch off Sam Masterson. Rip's got to work somewhere, and who else has offered it? Our fine friends on Clover Leaf? If so, I didn't happen to hear.'

Piper's lips were pinched, and Pick didn't care to start a family quarrel. Picking up the bridle reins, he said, 'Well, think it over, Rip. If your sister can open her mind a little, like your mother has, come over to Mesa and go to work. Then you'll be beholden to nobody at all.'

'He'll take the job,' the woman said, 'and you keep your mouth shut, Piper.'

Piper still strongly disliked the idea. She eyed her mother hotly, started to speak, then refrained. Turning, she walked stiffly into the house.

'That suit you, Rip?' Pick said.

'I reckon,' Rip said. He looked relieved that the choice had been made without his having to betray his own eagerness.

'I'll be over with spare horses tomorrow to get you and your personals.'

Rip tried to keep the wood in his cheeks, but a grin was trying to break through it.

Pick visited Josh Springs. By then the dead horse was offensive enough to keep away everything but the turkeynecked buzzards dotting the scene. They would have it carrioned off long before the cattle came out of the hills in the fall and needed the water. He rode from there to the ranch. He chored around headquarters until late afternoon, when the punchers came in. They had nothing untoward to report from their outriding. Pecos was the best cook in the group and so he made supper. Afterward the riders started a poker game, using beans for chips, and Pick joined in.

Then, around ten o'clock, a horse stitched its hoof sound through the outer night and stopped at the gallery steps.

'Somebody's in a rush,' Hosea said.

Getting up, Pick walked to the door and looked out to see Luke Gallatin fling himself from the saddle.

'Hello, Luke,' Pick called. 'What's up?'

'Something's gone wrong,' Luke said in a voice tight with concern. 'Mike never came down from the range this evening. I went up there and hunted around for him. I couldn't find a sign of him. I don't understand it, Pick, but Packwood's moved again.'

'What makes you think so?'

'Olive says yesterday she thought she saw somebody up there watching Mike from behind. She even had the impression he lined a rifle on Mike. But she's been upset. She figured it was her jumpy imagination and

99

never mentioned it. God, I wish she had. It might have saved Mike's life.'

'Take it easy, Luke. There could be some simple explanation.'

'It's Clover Leaf again,' Luke said doggedly, 'but it beats me why they picked on Mike. He hated them. He'd do anything to square things for my dad. But why'd they hit at him instead of me?'

'You think a lot of the old fellow, don't you?' Pick said.

'Like my own father.'

'If you're right, that could be it.'

'He's right,' Pecos said at Pick's elbow. 'Don't forget Hosea seen Hannegan on the pass road. He'd have crossed Luke's summer range to get there. He might have meant to kill Mike then and there, and Mrs. Gallatin scared him off.'

'Why'd he go on down to the pass, then?'

'Must have suspected he'd been seen and wanted to cover his tracks. By going out through the pass toward the Las Vegas road he could make it look like some saddle bum.'

Pick had to agree that the theory was at least plausible. It had convinced the others already. He saw the wrath in their eyes, the restlessness in their muscles.

He said, 'Keep hold of your tempers, boys. There's a chance something took Mike someplace that had nothing to do with Clover Leaf and he'll show up yet.'

'We gonna set on our hands and wait?' Blackie said.

'Till daylight. When there's enough light we'll go up and scout for sign. Luke, you get home to your wife. If she's alone she's scared.'

'She'd better be,' Luke said bitterly. 'Mike would have watched himself if she'd warned him. If they've hurt him she's to blame.'

'Cut that out,' Pick said sternly. 'She knows you're thinking that. She's thinking the same thing, herself. You get home and stand by her. We'll be over before daylight, and there's nothing to be done before then.'

Subsiding, Luke rode out.

The others went back indoors, but the poker game was forgotten. Pecos took a restless turn around the room, then stopped to look at Pick. 'What did you mean when you asked Luke if he didn't think a lot of Mike?'

'They could simply have latched onto him. Maybe to coerce Luke into withdrawing his support from me. Maybe to scare his wife with the idea that Luke will be next. If so, Mike's still alive and we've got a chance to get him back the same way.'

'How, if we don't ride in on Clover Leaf and force a showdown?'

'I don't know how,' Pick snapped. 'And we won't find out till we learn more of how it happened.'

He knew he was barely controlling his men. The outrageous killing of Tarrone and the attempt to frame Mesa for it had been hard enough to bear. Now a highly respected old man had vanished. They wanted action, to get at the roots of the thing.

The night wore on. No one slept and, after a time, no one said much except in a snapping, high-strung way. Pecos cooked breakfast in the last hours of night. Afterward they rode over to Big Springs, reaching there while the yellow shine of lamps still showed through the old trees.

Luke was waiting in the yard, a seething energy goading him. His horse was saddled and waiting. His voice slammed across the breaking day.

'We'll be able to see sign by the time we get up there. Let's ride.'

Pick saw nothing of Olive through the windows and open door. A deep pity stirred in him. Luke held her strictly to blame for failing to warn Mike of the danger to him. Even before then she had been a very unhappy woman.

'Olive up?' he said quietly to Luke.

Luke shrugged. 'Don't know. I haven't been indoors much tonight.'

'If you don't mind, I want to see her a minute.'

'Look—' Luke began, then his voice trailed off. 'Suit yourself.'

Pick dismounted and walked across the gallery to the open door. She sat across the room in a reading chair by a lamp and looked frayed and ill.

She said, 'Hello, Pick.'

'May I come in, Olive?'

She nodded and he walked on in, pulling off his hat. 'I suppose you feel like Luke does,' she said, 'and you're right. It's my fault.'

'Why is it?'

'I should have warned Mike.'

'Did you see enough to justify it?'

'That's the trouble,' she said in a despairing voice. 'It was just something there in the shadows and quite a ways off. The sun was on beyond. For an instant it seemed plain that it was a rider with a rifle pointed at Mike. Then it vanished completely. I've been nervous. I was pretty sure it was an optical trick. Luke's impatient with my fears, so I didn't say anything.'

'I know,' he said gently. 'I only hoped you could tell me something. You must have seen Hannegan a few times. Would you say this figure reminded you of him?'

'It was big, anyway.'

Pick nodded. 'That checks with some other things pointing to Hannegan. Quit blaming yourself, Olive. It's a mistake anybody could have made.'

She said very softly, 'But will Luke ever stop blaming me?'

'He's overwrought.'

'And fed up with me. I don't guess I blame

him, Pick.'

He could only touch her shoulder gently, then turn and walk out. There was a look of rocky inscrutability on Luke's face. He started his horse and, the others following, rode out.

Back of the home ranch the trail plunged at once into the lifts, following a short gorge, then breaking out onto the first high flat. Luke kept in the lead, knowing the vicinity intimately. He pressed on toward the lower edge of the far timber. They passed Big Springs cattle scattered across the range in typical bunches of eight or ten.

Reining in at the edge of the upper timber, Luke said, 'I left Mike here around five o'clock and went home. He was going to close the gate at Pine Spring so we could trap and brand some slick-ears. We better cover every foot from here to the spring.'

'Spread out, boys,' Pick said quietly.

They began to comb the slope for telltale signs of what had transpired up here after Luke left. They looked for suspicious horse tracks, an empty shell, evidence of someone's waiting or moving in stealth or, finally, of outright violence. They covered every foot of ground to Pine Spring without turning up a thing.

'Well, he made it to here,' Blackie said, nodding at the closed gate. A cut of whitefaces loitered outside the fence, impatiently waiting to get in to the water. Since there would be no branding done that day, he opened the gate and let the thirsty animals in to the spring's pooled water.

On a careful circle afterward, Pick let out a yell. Horse tracks still suggestively fresh indicated that Mike had gone on from the springs in this direction. When the others rode up to him Pick spoke tersely.

'Something drew him up that way.' He swung his head to stare at the timber.

'More than once,' Hosea said dolefully, 'I've cussed the fact that nothing can cross a piece of ground without leaving marks, not even me. This is once when I'm glad of it.'

They followed the sign to the edge of the timber, careful not to ride over and obliterate it. A short distance in, where the pines still stood at thin distances, they found what they hunted. A horse had waited in hiding in the cover of a brush-grown bank. Some kind of bait had been put out where Mike could see it from the spring. It had aroused his concern or simple curiosity and drawn him on in this direction voluntarily. That accounted for the lack of disturbing sign. There was still no evidence of a struggle, so he must have ridden into the threat of a gun. Mike had been forced to accompany the lurker away from there.

'He might still be alive,' Pick said encouragingly to Luke. 'I don't know how they got him up here. But I think the whole play's to get us to come after them, looking for blood. That, or to keep you from testifying against them in my favor.' He omitted mentioning that they might also have wanted to frighten Olive.

'If they want a visit from us,' Pecos said dangerously, 'why not let them have it?'

Hosea shook his head and surprised Pick by saying, 'Don't ever play the other fellow's game, friend. Make him play yours.'

Pick nodded. 'The fastest way I know is to make them trade Mike back, assuming they haven't killed him.'

'How could you do that?' Luke said.

'We'll take our own hostage and offer to swap. That would knock their denials and alibis in the head.'

'Who's so important to Packwood he'd give in?' Blackie said skeptically.

'Packwood himself. And he's got the money that gives the others their stake in this. If Mike's alive we've got to get him out of their hands before we can do anything else.'

'Then let's go after Packwood,' Pecos said.

Pick shook his head. 'It's a one-man job, and I'll handle it. It'll take a day or two, because I've got to catch him at Clover Leaf alone. But if Mike's alive the wait won't hurt him. If he's dead it won't hurt him, either.'

Again he had the feeling of trying to ride a volcano without a bridle. Through much of the night he had held them in check, angry, dynamic men whose main outlet was action.

Now he was asking them to wait longer. He eyed them coolly, steadily, letting their friendship and the respect they felt for him make their choice for them. It was the surprising Hosea who tipped the balance.

'You don't hatch eggs with a pile driver, boys. I guess we all know that.'

Even Luke nodded thoughtfully. They swung their horses and started down the slope toward the basin.

CHAPTER NINE

Piper failed to understand why, when she so thoroughly loathed Pick Atherton, she should feel a queer gratitude for a couple of things he had done. Wagon Tire was a much more pleasant place to be than Josh Springs. Sam's house was picturesque, comfortable, and clean. Now Rip was working, and that relieved a very real worry for her and her mother both.

She had not let herself believe for a moment that either action sprang from any kindness on Atherton's part. In the first instance, he had wanted them off Josh Springs and had simply moved them off arbitrarily. The job was an effort to soften them up so they wouldn't try to get back to Josh. He was a muttonhead if he thought she didn't see through it.

'I can tell when you're stewing about that fellow,' her mother said. 'Your face looks like you swallowed a polliwog.' She had washed and ironed all of Rip's clothes and was now patching them, seated in a barrel chair under a cottonwood. Piper lay on her back, looking up through the rustling leaves.

She said coldly, 'What fellow?'

'You know what fellow. You acted the headstrong spitfire. Now you've got to feel you were justified so you won't be ashamed.'

'Ashamed,' Piper said with a hoot. 'Even if

he never killed Pa, he's the one to be ashamed.'

Her mother glanced at her sharply. 'Why?'

'I never told you, but it was them spying on me while I took a bath that made me the maddest, that day.'

'You sure they did?'

Piper squinted an eye and looked up through the leaves. They hadn't tried to hide, and it wasn't likely they could have been there long enough to see her undressed without her catching on. But they had quietly watched her cavort and primp, which was nearly as bad. She made a sound that was neither denial nor affirmation.

Her mother looked at her musingly. 'I don't know that I'd hang them for it. A man takes pleasure in a pretty woman, and it's not always lust, either.'

'I'll believe that,' Piper said, 'when I see water run uphill.'

She sprang to her feet, impatient with all the attempts to convert her to a different way of thinking. Nonetheless there was a nagging question in her mind. Was shame partly responsible for her attitude and feelings? Their ill-concealed amusement when she discovered them had made her furious, reminding her of other times when she had felt men's eyes invading her privacy. Then had come that ordering-off, as if the Tarrones were tramps with no rights anywhere. So she had resorted to the rifle, and if that was being a headstrong spitfire she wasn't ashamed of being one.

Sam was off prospecting, or gophering, as he called it, and had taken Rip with him. A glance at the sun, the only clock she had ever known, told her they would soon be coming in hungry. That pleased her, for she hadn't had many real kitchens to cook in. She got kindling and wood from the big rick along the back wall and entered the house.

She had their supper ready to take up, when Sam and Rip came in together. She saw immediately that something was wrong, for the geniality was gone from Sam's face. He said nothing, and he and Rip washed at the bench beside the spring. Her mother came in to help her put the meal on the table.

'Something's troubling Sam,' she said. 'I wonder what it is.'

Piper looked at her quickly. 'I don't know, but I had the same feeling.'

Sam was an old-timer who drank coffee from a saucer and ate with a knife. Every tooth in his mouth was sound and white, and he had a hearty appetite. Her father hadn't had half his teeth left and had always complained of stomach trouble. Yet tonight Sam didn't attack his plate as usual.

'Well, miss,' he said finally, scowling at Piper, 'here's something for you to chew on. Me and Rip run into Pecos Benton. He says

Luke Gallatin's hired man is missing. Mike Terry. Him and me were the only real old-timers left. The sign shows pretty plainly Clover Leaf's either got him or have killed him.' He went on to recount fully what he had learned from Pecos.

'Now,' Rip said, 'let's hear you excuse Clover Leaf and blame Pick for that, too.' He had been won over completely by the job.

'You shut up,' Piper said.

But she had a reproof coming. Pick Atherton hadn't lied, and Sam hadn't been prejudiced in his favor. She realized that she had never truly believed that to be the case. Packwood had used them in an absolutely callous way. He had instigated the murder of her father. She had blinded herself to the plain truth because she had wanted his help so desperately.

She washed the dishes, slowly facing the fact that there was now no hope of staying in the Hueco. She hadn't realized until now how much she had wanted to stay. The reason was not solely the practical one of needing a living and wanting a home. It was much more elusive.

Except in a wild and often frightening way this was not attractive country. Yet she had sensed something in it that was necessary to her, something she would miss when they left. Rip could stay. He now liked Atherton and would want to keep his job. But there was no place for her and her mother unless she could help make a living. She would not impose on Sam's hospitality endlessly, and Rip was too young to be saddled with their full support. So they would trail on, and she would leave here something that had been strangely and mysteriously vital.

She was a controlled girl ordinarily and did not often give way to useless sorrow and regret. The day's light work was over, and she wanted something else to keep her occupied. Her mother had Rip's clothes ready for him to move to Mesa and didn't need her help. She felt contrite for having snapped at Rip.

She said, 'Want to go for a walk, Rip?' and smiled at him.

His expression lightened and he said, 'Sure.' They had always been close, although there was a four-year difference in their ages. They struck off together along the edge of the hills.

The day was going in the desert's swift way, the soft and wonderful tones of dusk replacing austerity with enchantment. Far to the southeast she could see the rearing formation she knew to be the landmark of Mesa Ranch. She knew that violent men lived over there, aroused now and preparing for new violence. The land fitted them and they fitted the land, and it came to her with a sharp, wise insight that she fitted the land and its men. She had known unrelieved ferocity that night at Josh Springs. She belonged in a place like this, with people like these. That was the thing she would miss.

They climbed onto a bald, rocky knob and presently seated themselves to rest. Out from them ran a corner of Mesa's range, empty now of stock with everything away in the mountains. A kind of excitement had crept into Rip's face as he stared outward with her, absorbed in his own thoughts.

Presently he said, 'Thirty a month adds up pretty fast when a fellow gets his keep thrown in. It'll take care of you and Ma, with something left over. After a while we could buy a steer or so.'

'There's no open land around here,' Piper said. 'There never was. Maybe Pa knew that and relied on Packwood to help him take it away from Mesa. I don't want to grab land from anybody. Do you?'

'I guess not,' Rip said, his excitement subsiding.

She rebelled in a quick, profound way against the need always to destroy their own dreams. That kind of hopelessness had made a mover out of their father, and she didn't want it to happen to Rip.

'I don't mean we can't have cattle pretty soon,' she said quickly. 'Maybe Ma and me can find a piece of land not too far off. We'll figure on that. You leave that to me and stay put, Rip. Don't get itchy-footed every time things don't go your way. That was Pa's trouble, and it was hard on Ma. Us too.'

He nodded. 'Sometimes a cowman lets a good hand run a few head on his graze. I heard a man tell Pa he got started that way. Some even brand slick-ears.'

'Rip,' she said, aghast.

'I wouldn't do that. But maybe if I work hard Pick'll let me take part of my wages in calves. Where'd you and Ma go, though?' He didn't like that part of it.

'Not far,' she promised. 'Ma wouldn't like that and I wouldn't, either.'

Night had closed about them, and they started back to Wagon Tire.

*   *   *

Pierce Hannegan rode out from Clover Leaf with a glint in his eyes that did not come from the bright sun. A while ago Abby Packwood had left on her morning ride. He was determined to let her know now that he was onto her and her treachery. To his mind she had cheapened herself enormously. Even a hard-bitten gun slinger of any pride gave a strict loyalty to his outfit. To do otherwise was mean and despicable, and he found pleasure in thus degrading her.

It was easy to follow her through the thin pine. He knew the range so well its runs were as familiar as the lines on his face. She liked to go up into the higher hills and drift along the ridges, where sweeps of the lower country opened to view from constantly changing angles. He had spied on her more than once and knew she sometimes stopped at such a viewpoint. She would leave her horse and sit for a great while, thinking her mysterious thoughts and content with her own company.

Although a big man, Hannegan rode lightly. He followed up through the thin pine of the slope, with the sun on his shoulders and throwing his shadow blackly forward. He watched the shadow distort itself this way and that, as he moved along with the horse.

He picked up Abby at the Two Braves rocks. He came in so quietly that when she turned to investigate she gave a marked start. She had dismounted but still held the reins of the horse. He ran a bold eye over the lines of her slender body as she stood there so stiff and proud. Habit made him touch his hat to her as he came up. He spoke mildly and knew she was not yet afraid of him. She had the protection befitting the boss's wife and relied on it.

He said, 'Good morning, Mrs. Packwood. Nice view from here. I always stop to take a look.'

She nodded coolly. He knew she was waiting for him to make his small exchange and get on with his business. He reached into his pocket and took out the makings and rolled a cigarette, slow with it.

'Would you happen to have a match?' he said finally, in a soft, courteous voice.

He saw the slim body stiffen. That one word and its associations had stirred her guilt. She narrowed her eyes. 'I don't carry them, Hannegan,' she said. 'I imagine you knew that.'

He smiled thinly, reached in a pocket and extracted his own match case. He lighted the smoke, his head held back, his own eyes watching her blandly.

'You might as well say it,' she said.

'Say what?'

'You're telling me you saw me go to Mesa and you know what I took there. What are you going to do about it, Hannegan?'

'Why not call me Pierce?' he murmured, and watched her face harden. 'I'd rather call you Abby. Off like this, of course.'

In a grimly angry voice she said, 'If my husband knew you were this fresh with me he'd kill you.'

'Who'd he kill if he knew you sold him out to Mesa?'

'If you tell him about that I'll say you lied and you'll be the one in trouble.' She knew he was playing her for thrills, was beginning to wonder what else he would try. 'You play the game of coercion badly, Hannegan. It won't get you a thing.'

'Wells banked a lot on that match case, Abby. Once I tell him what I saw, he won't

116

have any doubts who stole it. He knows I've never lied to him.'

After a moment she said, 'What's your price, Hannegan?'

He laughed. 'Tell you the next time we meet up here, Abby. Let's make that soon.'

Her initial bewilderment turned into shock, but she said nothing. He touched his hat with his exaggerated courtesy and rode on.

He had derived a deep thrilling from debasing her. Probably he would play her that way again, keeping her frightened yet mute and impotent. When he was tired of it he would tell Packwood for the pleasure of its effect on him.

CHAPTER TEN

Rip wasn't forgotten, although he might have thought so until Pick showed up at Wagon Tire around noon. Rip was waiting with an outward show of his former sullenness. He was dressed in clean overalls and shirt and had a ragged bedroll made up. Pick observed the contradictory signs in him, his ill-concealed excitement, and was secretly pleased. Mrs. Tarrone looked ill at ease but not unfriendly. Piper had ducked inside when he approached, although she might not know he had seen her. Sam seemed to be off somewhere, as usual.

Pick had brought three extra horses, two of them saddled to ride and a pony for a pack. The extra saddler had Rip and his mother curious, but he didn't explain it until they had lashed the boy's personals on the packsaddle. He pointed to the larger saddled horse and said, 'Climb aboard, Rip. He's yours.'

Rip took the reins and threw them over the horse's head, breaking into a grin that would no longer be repressed.

'Hoped Piper would be around,' Pick said. 'This little ginger boy has got too frisky. He needs a workout now and then, and I was hoping she'd give it to him.'

Mrs. Tarrone smiled then. 'It happens she's in the house. Piper, come out.'

Piper appeared in the doorway, her face stony. She looked only at her mother and said, 'Yes, Ma?'

When she wasn't answered she came down the steps. She knew what had been said and was interested but didn't want them to know it. Pick knew she liked the looks of the little horse where her glance strayed and fixed.

'I'm trying to get even with this butterball,' Pick said. 'Plez Brown's wife used to ride him, and I got him with the ranch. He's too light for a man, and loafing makes him onery and mischievous with the other horses. As a favor to them, I wish you'd take and work him.'

She nearly smiled. 'What's his name?' she said, and straightened out her face.

'What could it be but Ginger?'

She walked up to the horse and rubbed its muzzle with the flat of her hand. The horse liked it. Softly she said, 'Hello, boy.' Her eyes strayed to the saddle, which was a man's.

'Try him,' Pick said.

'I—I'm not dressed right.'

'All right if I leave him?' he said, and she nodded. 'All right, Rip. We've got work to do ourselves.'

'And you earn your hire,' Mrs. Tarrone said to her son, who nodded.

That was all. Impassively they separated.

Rip was silent throughout the ride to Mesa, and Pick didn't try to start a conversation. When they reached the ranch he turned the

119

boy over to Pecos, saying briefly, 'Let him ride with you a few days while he learns the ropes.'

Pecos looked Rip over dubiously but nodded. The boy's relief at passing the hard-bitten puncher's inspection was obvious. Pecos jerked his head and, carrying the roll, Rip followed him into the house.

Blackie and Hosea were at the corral where their saddled horses stood with slung necks. There was a look of gratification on Blackie's face.

'You've been looking for a tail hold on one of Packwood's squatters,' he said, 'and it looks like one come riding along.'

'How come?' Pick said.

Blackie tipped his head toward his elongated companion. 'Hosea, there. Seems he's got the Injun sign on Les Finney. We met up with Finney on the west bench. When he seen Hosea he looked like he'd ate a pail of bear grease.'

Pick shot the slim stranger a keen glance. 'You know Finney?'

'Sort of,' Hosea said. 'I told him one time if we ever met up again I'd kill him.'

'From his looks when they met,' Blackie said, 'Les sure remembers that.'

'You going to kill him?' Pick said.

'If he's around tomorrow. That's what I kind of told him this morning.'

'You must have a gun reputation.'

Hosea shook his head. 'Only for getting to

work on time when I've got to. This Finney, which ain't his name, don't have the nerve to face a man. Proved it some time ago. That particular country got crowded with him and me both in it. I so informed him. He got the idea, and the place got uncrowded.'

'Tell him how you feel about this country?'

'I allowed I'd arrived to stay and still liked room.'

Pick rubbed his jaw. It was time they got a break, and this could be it. What Hosea had said about Finney confirmed his own impression. But here the man had the power of the big Clover Leaf behind him. He might draw courage from that.

'Satisfy you if he just skins out again?' Pick said to Hosea.

'It'd suit me fine. I don't like killing.'

'Then, before Packwood's had a chance to stiffen the man's spine, I'm going to try to buy a quitclaim to his squatter's rights. It might hurry things if you'd come with me, Hosea.'

'Don't mind if I do,' Hosea said, and shoved to his feet.

They were soon in the canyon that lifted onto the mesa. Pick had prepared a deed and a draft on the bank in Rhyolite. The amount of the draft was a thousand dollars. If the offer was accepted that would be a cheap price for clearing Mesa's old rights to Gap Springs.

They reached Finney's shack in about an hour. Finney stepped out with a rifle in his hand. He looked scared, but the tough kind of scaredness that could be extremely dangerous.

'You two can get off my property,' he said in a toneless voice. There was no mistake about his knowing Hosea.

'Might as well put that thing down,' Pick said. 'You can't kill one of us without the other getting you. We're here to settle it without a fuss if you'll listen. Maybe Packwood could get you out of this and again maybe not. It's a gamble, and the stake's your life. Or have you practiced your draw to where you can beat this man now?'

'I ain't scared of him,' Finney said without conviction. 'Or of you, either.'

'Just the same, I'm offering you a thousand dollars and safe-conduct out of the country.'

'What for?'

'Your property and quitting your claim to the water you grabbed from Plez Brown.'

Finney's heated eyes riveted on Pick, then swung to stare at Hosea. 'This is a put-up job,' he blazed. 'You got hold of him somewhere and brought him here.'

'If so, I'm being generous. With you dead I wouldn't need your quitclaim and I'd save a thousand dollars.' He produced the draft. 'Ride through Rhyolite, and the bank will honor this.'

The defiance was leaking out of Finney under the impact of Hosea's eyes and the cold logic in what Pick had said. That old trouble must have been serious, for Hosea's face was anything but good-humored now. Finney tried to muster another protest; then abruptly his shoulders sagged.

Tipping his head at Hosea, he said, 'You see he lets me get out of the country?'

'I guarantee it.'

'Then—all right.'

Finney lowered the rifle but still would not let go of it, his eyes prowling steadily to Hosea. He accepted the papers and stubby pencil Pick handed him and scribbled his signature. The thousand dollars was a just price for his few head of cattle, his extra horses, and the knocked together equipment on the ranch. His outfit had never been anything but a blind, and he might even still owe Packwood for the steers.

When Pick had the signed deed in his hand he said, 'Now saddle and get. And if there's a trick, Finney, I'm taking the leash off this fellow.'

Finney was thoroughly impressed by then with the deadliness of his situation. He made up a roll, saddled a horse, and rode out through the gap.

'Suit you?' Pick said to Hosea.

'Like oysters for supper. What're you going to do with his layout now you've got it?'

'It's still what it always was. A part of Mesa Ranch.'

'Packwood won't try to squat another man

123

here?'

'He won't dare once he knows about this.' Pick waved the deed. 'And I aim to do business with him next.'

'When?'

'In the morning, after his crew's rode out on the work. He don't go with them usually.'

Hosea grinned. 'This deal puts Reedy Smith on a hot seat. Mesa's between him and Clover Leaf now. Think we could work it on him?'

'Not unless you've got the Injun sign there, too.'

'Don't happen to,' Hosea said regretfully, 'but it might be easier to get one now.'

'We'll try. And thanks for the help.'

Hosea's eyes had mellowed again, and Pick knew he had sound and loyal help in this strange man from nowhere. The West was full of his kind, strays whose records wouldn't stand close inspection but who lived by strangely admirable codes in most respects.

First light, the next morning, found Pick on Stud Knob, immediately overlooking Clover Leaf. His horse was hidden back in the rocks, and he sat where he was himself blended into their shadows, watching the sky over the far Piutes come afire with daylight.

He saw smoke start from the cookshack chimney. The wrangler rode into the big pasture to bring in the remuda. Afterward men appeared in the yard, stirred out of the bunkhouse by the foreman. They entered the cookshack in a rush when the triangle sounded, and presently the day horses bucketed in. Pick kept his vigil for another hour before the last of the riding force had saddled and gone.

He was certain that yesterday they had kept pretty well bunched on the chance of action from Big Springs and Mesa as a result of Terry's disappearance. But ranch work always pressed, and now the outfit was being forced back into routine as Pick had expected. That had been the basis for his patient waiting. When the last rider had been swallowed by the hills he went to his horse. He stepped across and came off the knob into the brush back of the ranch buildings.

He rode quietly until he was behind the stables, where he dismounted and left the horse. A short move took him around the end of the building. From there he could slip in to the ranch house without being seen from the kitchen by the cook. As he looked he froze in his tracks. Wearing a riding skirt and carrying a quirt, Abby Packwood came out of the house's back door and started toward the corral.

She saw him off to the side, and her eyes rounded. For a moment they locked with his, a look of deep curiosity on her face. Then, still silent, she moved on to the corral and was lost from sight. Pick stood motionless, his heart knocking hard in his chest. She couldn't help knowing that his intentions here were not peaceable and was letting him have his way. He waited until he heard her ride out.

That left no one to worry about immediately but the cook and Packwood himself. Pick slid on to the back wall of the office jutting from the end of the house. He ducked under the window, drew his gun, and stepped through the open door.

'Take it easy, Packwood,' he said softly to the man at the desk, 'or you're dead.'

Wells Packwood looked up in amazement. Color climbed above the open neck of his shirt.

'You,' he said in a heavy breath. 'What're you doing here?'

'Keep the voice down and stand up. If you've got a gun in that desk don't try for it.'

Packwood pushed up from his chair, his face livid. Pick ordered him back, stepped in, and opened the center drawer of the paper-strewn desk. His free hand came out with a Colt .45. He moved back, jamming the extra gun under his belt.

'Now set down again, Packwood, and take a pen. Write a note for Hannegan to see when he comes in at noon. Say I've got you and he's only got till dark tonight to swap Mike Terry for you. You won't be at Mesa, but he can make contact with me there.'

'Terry?' Packwood said with a gasp. 'What have we got to do with him?'

'Never mind the eyewash. Write what I told

126

you.'

With a helpless motion of the hands Packwood said, 'I don't know what you're driving at. Do you expect Hannegan to latch onto old Terry for you? I wouldn't know why, but if so, this is a crazy way to go about it.'

'If you don't know what the note means, Hannegan will. Write it out.'

With an angry shrug Packwood sat down again and wrote for a moment. Pick satisfied himself that he had been obeyed and propped the note against the inkwell. Then he ordered the man toward an inside door that opened into the main house. Coming behind, he kept his gun jammed in the small of Packwood's back. The rancher seemed to realize his wife had left. He tramped out through the house in indifference, not expecting anybody to intercede for him.

They moved across the yard the same way Pick came. At the end of the stables he told Packwood to rope and saddle a horse, warning him he would be shot if he made a false move. He stood concealed from the cook's view but with his gun on Packwood. The rancher stepped into the trap with a rope. His temper still goaded him, but he was soon ready to ride. Pick motioned him up. When they were both cut off from the cookshack Packwood made another plea.

'What you're demanding's impossible,' he said bitterly. 'You'll only bring my men down on you.'

'Get going,' Pick said, nodding toward the near draw in the hills.

In about an hour, when he realized they were angling into Gap Springs, Packwood began to show curiosity. 'If you think Finney might help you get out of this,' Pick said, 'he's left the country. He quit his claim and sold me his haywire outfit. I've got the deed to prove it.'

Packwood looked stunned. 'When?'

'Yesterday. He's long gone now.'

Blackie waited at the springs. He grinned when Pick rode in with the prisoner. Pick turned Packwood over to him, saying, 'Hold onto him and shoot him if he gives you half a reason.'

'Fourth of a reason is all I need,' Blackie said.

After a long frowning look at Packwood, Pick said, 'You were pretty insistent about not being able to produce Mike Terry. There's only one reason you couldn't, Packwood. Is he dead?'

From the look that leaped onto Packwood's face Pick had a sagging fear that he had hit the mark. They could trade a live man but not a dead one without confessing to his murder.

Blackie's voice was dangerous. 'You heard what he asked, Packwood. Is Mike dead?'

'I don't know a thing about him, I tell you.'

Hoping his hunch was mistaken, Pick rode

128

on. It was mid-morning when he reached. Mesa. The other riders were still out on their morning work. There was nothing to do now but await contact with Hannegan. That could come any time between noon and night and in any form.

CHAPTER ELEVEN

Olive was about to mount her private horse when Sam Masterson rode in through the cottonwoods at Big Springs. They rarely saw the old prospector, whom Luke called a hermit, but when Sam discerned her he angled his old nag toward her readily. Upset as she was, she was pleased by the respectful way he pulled off his hat to her.

'Howdy, Mrs. Gallatin. Luke around anywhere?' he said.

'He's up with the cattle, Mr. Masterson.'

Sam looked disappointed. 'Well, I was scared of that. The Mesa boys are all off somewhere, too. Things are getting bad around here, ma'am. I figured I better have another man along for what I've got to do.'

'Could I help you?' Olive said impulsively, wanting to please him as he had her.

Sam looked at her, thoughtful and a little surprised. 'It might not be nice, if my hunch is right. Pecos told me about Mike. Come to me in the night I once dug a prospect hole in the Piutes. I aim to take a look at it.'

Olive felt the old queasiness in her stomach. 'You think they've killed him? I've been hoping—' She left the sentence incomplete.

Sam nodded grimly. 'Minute I heard about it I knew old Mike's done for. Take a look at what happened to Tarrone. It's the way that bunch works. They know about my old prospect. It's on what's now part of their summer range. It was a likely ledge, but when I explored I hit water and had to quit. It stands half full. Just right for their purpose.'

Olive broke in urgently. 'Let me go with you, Mr. Masterson. I so want to help.'

If they could find Mike, even dead, it might put an end to the emotion crowding Luke into dangerous action against Clover Leaf. But it would never lessen his bitterness at her failure. She knew that with the certainty that told Sam, Mike was dead.

'I better try and find Luke,' Sam said.

'That would be miles out of your way. I want to do it. Please.'

'All I need is a witness if I locate Mike,' he mused. 'That Clover Leaf bunch is tricky. But- no. Tomorrow'll have to do.'

'We've got to find out now.'

'Well, if you can stomach it I'd sure like to see.'

'I can.'

Olive footed a stirrup and swung up before he changed his mind. One thing at which she had succeeded at Big Springs was learning to ride like an expert. The doctor had warned her against it at present, but she was doing it anyway, not caring what happened to her. Sam swung his horse and pointed the way toward the foot slope of the Piutes.

'Pecos told me the sign led into the high pass and down the other side,' Sam said. 'That's what they'd do. If they've got to alibi they'll claim it was a saddle tramp that done Mike in to get his horse and money. They could cut the Vegas road and lose the tracks in the travel. Then they'd come back to my old prospect through another notch in the range and get rid of the body. I'd bet my life that's what happened.'

'I never knew people could be so utterly beastly.'

'Well, it's a tough country that calls for tough people. But nobody needs to go as far as they do.'

Olive wondered why she so lacked the capacity for growing tough herself. She hadn't realized it, but it might have been fear that really kept her from investigating when she saw the mounted man spying on Mike. Whatever; it had destroyed the last hope of matters between her and Luke being righted. She still had not told him about the baby. They had started quarreling when she came home, and she couldn't bear to reveal such news under circumstances like that. Now she wouldn't even if she stayed here, letting him discover it for himself.

Sam struck a faded trail that Big Springs had used before it lost this part of the range to Clover Leaf. It climbed off the greasewood bottom and up to where sage appeared with scrub oak and nut pine. The heat lessened. Above the ridge line ran a sky broken by a single cloud that looked lost and lonely. Presently Sam put his horse into a gorge that climbed steeply for a great distance beside a trickling stream. They topped out in another of the country's long high valleys.

She saw, off to the left and glaring in the sun, the naked rock of a ledge toward which Sam headed. Her throat tightened, but she kept her fear from bursting out and rendering her helpless. As they drew closer she saw a heap of tailings and the rotted skeleton of a winch that once had stood over the prospect. She saw Sam's wondering glance come toward her, then he looked back at the prospect, and they rode up. She kept saddle while the old man slid off the nag and stood stitching a keen inspection across the sandy ground.

'Horse tracks,' he said, nodding his head. 'Not very old, either. You making out all right?'

Olive nodded, the scratching feeling back in her throat and her stomach heavy.

Sam walked up to the prospect, a shaft driven down like a well, where he had once investigated an outcrop. He looked around, moved to the tumbled-over winch, and twisted loose an upright. He began to poke this into the hole. Once he brought up the heavy pole, and she saw that its end was wet. She loathed watching, yet at the moment could not have torn her eyes away from that prospect. It would determine her fate as it might already have determined Mike's.

Sam began to probe again and finally brought his pole to rest on the edge of the bank and bore down on his end. After a moment he quit and scrubbed a gnarled brown hand over his face.

Looking up at Olive, he said, 'Brought him to the surface for a second. At least, somebody.'

She grasped the saddle horn for the whole landscape dipped and teetered. This left her, and she saw that Sam had pulled up his probe and dropped it on the ground.

'Take hooks,' he said. 'Shaft's too deep for a man to get down there and heave him out. But now we know.'

'Now we know,' she said in a dead voice.

Sam flung a keen look along the open meadow. 'Don't reckon we've been seen, but you never can tell. If so, they might fish him out and move him. So I got to bring him up again enough to identify, and there I got to have the witness. Think you can do it?'

She nodded and numbly got down from the horse. It took longer that time for Sam to surface what he sought. Twice she saw something barely break water, but the something was obviously a man's back. Sam kept on doggedly, and all at once they both saw the ghastly face of Mike Terry. She couldn't restrain a torn, sick outcry. Then the muddy water enfolded the body again, and Sam brought up the pole. He looked a little sick himself.

'They weighted him,' he said. 'If I hadn't got to thinking on this old ledge he'd never have been found. We better git now, and you're a mighty plucky woman.'

How she wished that were true. Then she might live through the moment when they told Luke what had happened because of her failure.

*   *   *

Pierce Hannegan was blowing his horse in the shade of Papoose Head when he saw a woman riding along the edge of the hill-locked flat far below him. For a moment he regarded the sight puzzledly, for women were scarce in the Hueco. Then he recognized the Clover Leaf horse as it drew nearer and was all attention. Abby was out very early and riding in a direction she never chose because it ran into country where he and his men were usually at work.

Ahead of her ran the interlocking meadows of the Hueco Hills, into which he had just fanned his riders on the day's routine. He was himself bound for the Clover Leaf cow camp on the south edge of the hills. He finished his cigarette and was about to ride on when his gaze, returned to Abby down there, riveted in closer observation. She was turning away from the regular trail through the hills, the easiest riding, and making toward a rough draw cutting to the southeast. As this brought her yet nearer, he discerned the saddlebags behind her saddle, and suspicion squirmed through his mind.

He had taken his secret delight in letting her know he was onto her unfaithfulness and throwing his own scare into her. It simply had not entered his head that she might try to clear out. Those saddlebags strongly suggested an intention to travel, and she could be making for the railroad at Las Vegas, toward which the southeastern draw would head her.

He let her get off the flat and into the draw, then put his horse in motion, swinging along the ridge above her. If that fine-feathered fowl thought she was flying the coop she had another think coming. He ran his horse swiftly through the scrub. When he was well ahead of her he angled off the ridge and into the draw, where he pulled up and waited.

It was five minutes later when she came around a point of rocks and saw him. Her horse hauled up. Hannegan would have been satisfied had she whirled and bolted, aware that he was onto her again and would not let her run away from it. She surprised him by coming straight on.

'A mite off the beaten track, ain't you,

Abby?' he said roughly.

Her eyes were very level and very cool. 'Aren't you?'

'Just happened to notice you and the saddlebags. How come?'

Her back stiffened even more, and he was aware of the color on her neck and cheeks. Her eyes still met his, carrying a surprising impact. He realized she wouldn't back down from him.

'Who gave you authority to question me, Hannegan?' she said.

'What I know about you is authority enough.'

She started to ride on, passing him, but he reached out and grasped the cheek strap of her horse's bridle. Her quirt came up and struck his arm a stinging blow, making him let go. Her objecting horse arced around and began to snort, widening the distance between them.

Grasping his pain-shot arm, Hannegan ripped out an oath.

'Stay away from me,' she said in a low, clear voice. A gun had come out of her skirt pocket and was in her hand.

'If you think you're getting out of it, you little tramp,' Hannegan said furiously, 'you're crazy.'

'Ride out of here, Hannegan, or I'll shoot you out of that saddle.'

He sat with heaving breath. He had looked

at death before and he saw it again, very close.

'Ride,' she said, and Hannegan turned his horse and headed down the draw.

He cut a look back just before he vanished beyond the point of rocks. She still sat watching him. After letting the one chance pass there was no use trying to get ahead of her again. He would tell Packwood at once what he knew about her. Packwood could take it from there.

It was around ten o'clock when he rode into the Clover Leaf yard. Swinging down in front of the office, he saw through the window that Packwood was not at the desk where he spent most of his mornings working on the ranch books. A glance at the corral told him also that the rancher's favorite horse was gone.

Hannegan walked over to the cookshack. 'Know where the boss went?' he asked.

'Never seen him leave,' the cook said. 'Ain't he in his office?'

'Might be in the house,' Hannegan said.

Packwood wasn't there, although Hannegan opened the door and went through the house. He came back into the office by way of the inside door. Shrugging, he was about to leave when he saw a piece of paper propped against the inkwell on the desk. Walking around, he saw that it was a note left for him.

His eyes went narrow and cold as he read it: 'Pierce—— Atherton's taking me and says he's holding me till you turn Mike Terry over to

138

him. Bring Terry to Mesa before night.' That was all, but it was plenty.

Hannegan felt his pulse flatten into an almost unbroken run. Only he and Packwood knew what had happened to Terry, that he couldn't be produced without hanging them both. Hannegan wondered why he had left such a crazy message. Then he realized that the words were Atherton's, dictated at gun point and put down by Packwood. A great rage shook Hannegan, driving out of his head all thought of the escaping woman.

When the initial reaction quit jolting him he began to realize the seriousness of his plight. He had to get Packwood out of Mesa's hands at once and without complying with the ultimatum. Afterward they could suspect and be damned. Clover Leaf would stick to the theory that some desperado had wanted Terry's horse and killed him to avoid spreading an alarm, disposing of the body. Eventually fear and worry would bring Luke Gallatin to time.

It had seemed a foolproof scheme to Hannegan when he carried it out. Now he wondered what progress Atherton would make to prove it otherwise. The man had to be taken care of, or there was little hope of dominating Gallatin. Hannegan set to work, pacing the floor while he figured out the move. Presently he walked out, mounted his horse, and rode down into Hueco Basin.

He wanted help, and with his men scattered far south of headquarters the closest place to get it was Les Finney's. He reached the line fence and followed it, his trotting horse kicking up the thick dust of the road. He left the lane at the end of the playa and cut a slant toward the squatter's shack under the brown rolls of the Drys.

His shout failed to bring Finney into the yard, but Hannegan rode on up to the steps, calling out again.

'Rattle out here, Les. I need help.'

When there was no answer he rode to the end of the house. There he could see the pole corral angled out from the closed-in shed that made a stable of sorts. The corral was empty, but what captured Hannegan's interest was the fact that the shed door was closed tight, something Hannegan had never seen. Finney was lazy and slovenly when it came to honest chores. A faint suspicion wormed through Hannegan's brain. He flung another look at the shack, then rode on north toward Reedy Smith's setup.

Around a rocky point he reined in and, stepped out of the saddle, his heavy face pinched. It was the work of a minute to make his way back along the cut-bank that ran behind the Finney layout. He came in on the rear of the stable and took a look through one of the yawning cracks in the wall.

What he saw electrified him—Packwood's

horse and another that wore the Mesa iron. He didn't understand what had happened to Finney. But the sheer chance of wanting his help had brought him to where they were holding Packwood. Maybe Atherton was in there with him and could be dealt with summarily.

There was a surer way to go about it than trying to storm the shack or sneak in on it by himself. Returning to his horse he mounted hastily and rode on to Reedy Smith's.

Instead of tall and skinny as his name suggested, Smith was a squat man, blocky in stature. He listened with growing interest to what the Clover Leaf foreman told him.

'You go in like I did,' Hannegan said in conclusion. 'As if it was an ordinary visit. Yell for Finney and keep their attention on the front of the place. I'll sneak in the back way and get the jump on the Mesa rooster.'

'Let's go,' Smith said eagerly. Like Finney, he was more interested in excitement than in the tedium of daily work.

Reflecting, Hannegan said, 'Whoever it is, he'll have his gun on Packwood to keep him quiet. He won't answer, either. So when you've yelled a couple of times go onto the porch like you were coming in.'

'And get myself shot?'

'By then I'll be set to handle it.'

Having returned with Smith, Hannegan halted at the rocky point as before. 'Wait here five minutes,' he said. 'Then go in.' He plunged into the brush underskirting the bluff.

Excitement was high in him by then, a sure confidence. He slid in behind the shed and paused to see if he had caused any commotion. Only silence came back to him. He waited there, intently listening for Smith's first shout. When it came he went in a bent run toward the shack's back door.

Smith's second call racketed to him. 'Les, you home?'

Hannegan came up to the back of the shack and paused, his shoulders pressed to the wall. There was no sense risking his life until he was sure those inside had their attention fixed firmly on the front of the house. Then he heard Smith pounding, moved to the nearby door with a drawn gun, and gently swung the door inward.

As he expected, Packwood was there under a gun. But the man with him was Blackie Chase. Both still watched the front, unaware of him. In this second of discernment Hannegan began to empty his gun into Chase.

The puncher only got half turned around before his arms flung upward and his knees collapsed. The sound of the shots jarred the shack and rapped off the outside bluffs. Packwood had jumped aside to get out of range. There was a look of incredulous relief on his blanched face.

In the sudden silence the rancher said, 'By

damn, Pierce, that was a smart piece of work.'

Hannegan saw that a couple of his shots had drilled the thin door. Stepping over Chase, he yanked the door open. Reedy Smith lay sprawled on the ground below the step in a pool of blood. Hannegan dropped down, bent, and lifted the man's arm. It fell back limply.

Looking up at Packwood, Hannegan said, 'The damned fool didn't know enough to get out of the line of fire.'

Packwood looked at the dead squatter with indifference, although he might have guessed that Smith had been used ruthlessly to ensure the success of Hannegan's scheme. He said, 'Let's get out of here.'

CHAPTER TWELVE

Pick listened in rising fury to what Sam had come to Mesa to tell him. It was hardly a surprise to learn for sure that Mike Terry was dead, but the utterly heartless way the crime had been committed offended his every decent instinct. 'You say Olive went to tell Luke?' he said, knowing what a dreadful duty that would be for her.

Sam nodded. His face had turned into the sharp, belligerent face of a hawk. His voice was gruff, and his old eyes held a mixture of anger and sorrow. 'I wanted to do it, but she insisted it was her place.'

'She feels to blame for it, Sam.'

'Why?' When Pick had explained more fully the circumstances leading to Mike's death Sam shrugged and let out a weary sigh. 'Well, I wouldn't call it her fault, and I guess you can't blame Luke. Pity, too. She strikes me as a fine little woman.'

'One of the best,' Pick said, 'but that doesn't make them suited to each other.'

Sam snorted. 'They better get suited. I don't know about the more comfortable places. I never lived in one long. But I know this country. It don't bend itself to nobody. They bend to it, or they're dead.'

'I think she's trying.'

'I don't mean her alone,' Sam said irritably. 'I mean Luke, too. They both got to bend themselves to suit their marriage and stop expecting it to bend to suit them.'

'Well, she took her turn bending him to her. Maybe when he's tired of his turn they'll get together. But that won't even have a chance to happen if we don't get on top of this new move of Packwood's. Their play for Josh backfired, and it's pretty plain they've moved their sights to Big Springs. If they can knock it out of the fight one way or another, it would be easier to finish off Mesa.'

Sam nodded his agreement.

Taking a restless turn along the gallery, Pick knew his grip on Packwood had been weakened, if not destroyed, by the discovery of Mike's body. Now Clover Leaf would deny any involvement whatsoever, charge an unwarranted abduction of Packwood, and proceed to make capital from it. So they had to be kept from learning of the discovery as long as possible.

'Look, Sam,' he said, 'we'd best get the authorities out here on the quiet and let them take care of Mike. It's better for them to see and have more than our word for it, anyway. I'll get a man off to Long String to telegraph Sunderleaf. Meanwhile I've got a scheme on with Clover Leaf. I still could get somewhere with it if we keep this from them a while.'

Sam agreed, swung onto his horse, and left.

Pick moved restlessly about the house. It was after two, with no sign of Hannegan in response to the ultimatum. Possibly he hadn't seen the note from Packwood yet. Or maybe he was on some maneuver of his own, a prospect that now made this idle waiting intolerable. He was up against men so ruthless he couldn't trust his own logic about them or his predictions of their conduct.

He waited another hour, then, impatiently clapping on his hat, went over to the corral and saddled a horse. At the gap leading onto the west bench he saw Pecos and Hosea coming across the bottom from Josh Springs, Rip with them. He waited until they rode up to him.

He told them briefly what Sam and Olive had found at the old prospect in the Piutes, concluding, 'Get something to eat and a fresh horse, Pecos, and hit for Long String. I'm going over to check on Blackie at Les Finney's shack.'

'Maybe I better go along with you,' Hosea said.

'If you like.'

Pecos rode on toward the ranch with Rip, while Pick and Hosea struck up into the gap. They crossed the bench and were nearly over the playa when Pick pointed forward. A horse with dragging reins was grazing a short distance this side of Finney's shack.

'That nag belongs to Reedy Smith,' he said.

'What's it doing there?'

'Let's find out,' Hosea said, and struck his horse with his spurs.

They rode forward at a gallop, coming in on the squatter's place. Pick saw the open door and realized what it was he saw on the ground by the step. He swung out of the saddle and ran forward, passing Smith's body and bounding up the step. Astounded and chilled, he stared down at the bullet-riddled body of Blackie. The open back door told him a little of the story.

'How did they know where I brought Packwood?' he said in a gasp.

'They sure seem to have known.' Hosea had withdrawn the gun near the dead puncher's hand and broken it open. 'Somebody sneaked in the back way and pumped Blackie full of lead. Smith was holding his interest in the front, and Blackie never exploded a shell.'

'Then who killed Smith?'

The question answered itself when they looked at the door splintered from inside.

'Accident,' Hosea said, 'and the only halfway break Blackie had. It at least took one of them with him.'

Still puzzled as to how Hannegan had caught onto it so quick, Pick remembered his encounter with Abby Packwood outside the Clover Leaf house. It would account for this but seemed incredible after her visit to Mesa bringing Luke's match case. No, something else had happened to put Hannegan wise.

They went back outdoors, still aghast at what they had found here on top of the proof of Mike Terry's death. Pick felt the loss of old friends and saddlemates more deeply than did Hosea, a newcomer. Yet the thin man's face was set in an icy cast. Few men could see a bullet-riddled back and not want to do something about it summarily.

'Well?' Hosea said in a flat voice.

'Don't lose your head, Hosea. They're going to tell the law that I grabbed off Packwood and they had to rescue him and Blackie got killed in the fight. So we'll have to be careful what we do next. I did grab Packwood and I'm already under suspicion about Tarrone. They might wind up making hay out of this.'

'More than one man's raked up a rattler in his hay. We'd better see that's the case now, or they'll have the whole basin.'

Pick agreed.

He knew it could be several days before the sheriff reached the basin again. These dead men could not be left like this in the heat, although he would have liked Sunderleaf to see precisely what he and Hosea had found. The best thing would be to send the bodies to the undertaker, but he was already left with no help but Hosea's and what Rip could give. He decided to ask Sam to witness this scene, then bury the bodies.

They got blankets from the bunk in the

house and covered the dead men. Pick left Hosea there and rode down to Wagon Tire Well. He found Piper at the spring, where she had come for a pail of water. For the first time she gave him a greeting and a shy smile.

'Hello, Pick,' she said.

'What took the pepper out of you?' he said.

'Sam told us about that poor old cowboy. I've been so wrong, Pick.'

'If you're finally right, that's what really counts.'

'I never thanked you for letting me use Ginger. He's a dandy little horse. And about Rip. I know you only hired him to help us out.'

'Not altogether,' Pick said. 'Rip's got the right stuff. Once he's learned his job he'll make a top hand.'

She looked at him earnestly. 'You really think that? I've worried. Some ways he was a little like Pa.'

'And in some ways like you. Which is the side I'm betting on, Piper.'

Her eyes widened. 'Then you don't think I'm so awful?'

'I never did think so. But I come to see Sam. He at the house?'

She nodded and he rode on.

Sam was eating a meal, Mrs. Tarrone there gossiping with him, but he shoved back instantly when he heard what Pick had to say. They rode back to Gap Springs, where Sam made note of the circumstances. Pick felt that

Sam's word, the word of the most impartial man in the basin, would carry weight against the fiction Clover Leaf would invent. They buried the dead men under the cottonwoods and went back to Wagon Tire.

Studying Piper a moment, Pick said, 'You still want a piece of land to settle on?'

'Not somebody else's,' she said. 'I learned my lesson.'

'Josh Springs wasn't open, but this piece is. Reedy Smith's squat claim. At the moment it's vacant.'

'Sam says that belongs to Mesa, too.'

'Correct. But if we move onto it ourselves it'd be playing Packwood's game. He'd say we killed Smith for it. On the other hand, he'll have his own man there again if somebody don't occupy it fast.'

Piper's mouth had dropped open as she listened. 'Are you suggesting that we move there?'

'Right away. Packwood wouldn't dare touch you after the fuss he made about the treatment you got at Josh Springs. Rip's wages'll keep you going, and this fall I figure to bring in a new herd. I'd like you folks to run some for me on shares.'

There was a look of wonder in Piper's eyes. 'You're serious. You really want us to do it,' she said in a strange, awed voice.

'The only question is—will you?'

'Oh—yes.'

150

Tears welled in her eyes, and he knew it was at the prospect of pulling her own oar at last. Yet what he offered would be as much a help to Mesa as to the homeless family. It would be a big step toward rolling Clover Leaf out of the basin.

'I hate to lose your company,' Sam said to Piper, 'but he's got the right idea. Let's get at it before Clover Leaf beats us to the jump.' He grinned. 'By damn, you cleaned that mangy outfit off the whole foot of the Drys. I like it a lot better.'

'If we make it stick,' Pick said.

It wasn't much work to load the Tarrones' few possessions in the wagon. While they were doing it Hosea hitched the scrawny team to the dish-wheeled vehicle. Afterward Piper drove the horses, Pick, Hosea, and Sam outriding her. By early evening the derelict family was settled in a new home, one it could call its own at last. Pick offered to advance Rip's first month's wages so Piper and her mother could drive to Long String and stock up. Meanwhile Sam and Mesa Ranch would loan them what they needed.

From the look in Piper's eye and his memory of how she had stood against him at Josh Springs he knew Clover Leaf would have trouble objecting to this move even if it decided to reverse its attitude about their rights. He rode back to Mesa with Hosea, feeling that some good had come from the developments in which Blackie had given his life. He knew Blackie would like it so, that the tough man of the desert might rest easier now.

When they came to the edge of the playa Pick stopped his horse. For a long moment he stared at the fence Smith had so insolently built out from the dry rimrock to shut Mesa stock off its rightful range.

Reaching for his catch rope, Hosea said, 'If you're thinking what I am, let's get it out of there.'

'We'll more than rip it out,' Pick said. 'We're going to move it up past Gap Springs and shut Packwood in the hills.'

'When?'

'What's wrong with tonight? All we've got to do is cross the bay that runs into his headquarters. Only a few hours' work.'

Hosea shot a look toward the far hills, growing misty in the dusk. He grinned, seeing as Pick did that the maneuver would contain the Clover Leaf cattle where they were at present, inside and south of the hills.

'Maybe that's the rattler in the hay,' Hosea said.

Rip was at headquarters, and it pleased Pick to see that he had gone ahead and got supper started. Rip said that Pecos had left for Long String right after noon. When Pick told him his family had moved to a place of its own Rip choked up. He was more than ready to put in an extra shift on the fence that night.

They waited until after dark, then loaded the needed tools into the buckboard, hitched horses, and drove out to the end of the doomed fence. Pick put Rip to pulling staples and rolling up the strands of wire. He and Hosea used a wagon jack to prize up the pointed posts. This turned up many times the material they needed for the relocated line, but Pick wanted the old fence entirely removed. The extra posts and wire were piled under the rim at the west end of the old line. Around two in a starlighted morning they drove south for the second step.

When they came to the edge of the bay into the hills they began to unload posts and wire at intervals. Still the night held no disturbance, although they had moved much closer to Clover Leaf. Using a wooden maul, they began to drive in posts, wondering how far the heavy chunking would carry through the silent night.

'Going to leave 'em a Texas gate?' Hosea said when they came to Clover Leaf's main road to the gap. That was a short section of wire cut so it could be laid back to open the fence.

Pick nodded. 'We'll give them no excuse to rip the whole thing out.'

They pressed on urgently, tension bothering them, all sending an occasional uneasy glance to the south. It seemed a long while before the last post was driven in. Stringing the wire kept them humping until nearly daylight, but it was a less noisy job. When the last staple was driven in, Pick wiped his brow with a sigh.

'The law's on our side in this,' he said as they loaded the tools. 'I've got a deed from Finney for the land we've run the fence on. Packwood's always insisted Finney was the rightful owner. He can't tear out the fence without reversing himself there, too. But we can't bet he won't. They're taking bigger chances all the time.'

'Tangle a man in his own rope long enough,' Hosea said, 'and you might get him hog-tied.'

They climbed into the buckboard and rolled out for home.

Rip's growing body was logged with fatigue, and even the wiry Hosea looked droopy-eyed. When they had eaten breakfast Pick told them to get a little sleep and stretched out on his own bed. Yet the tensions wouldn't let go, and he only dozed. He was up in about an hour, drank more coffee, and saddled a horse. He struck off across the big meadow toward the Gallatin ranch.

Only Olive was at headquarters and she said Luke was still up on the range. The girl's lined face filled Pick with concern.

'You had a bad experience, Olive,' he said gently. 'But you mustn't let it prey on your mind.'

'I'll never forget it or my part in it,' she said in a dull voice. 'And neither will Luke.'

'Nobody could know they'd hit at Luke

through Mike.'

'But why did they do it?'

'What does Luke think?'

She looked at him, miserable and badgered. 'He hasn't spoken to me since I told him about Mike.'

Pick rubbed his jaw, understanding Luke's feelings but realizing how unfair it was to Olive. He had meant to tell Luke of the new trouble at Gap Springs but knew that she had had enough of tragedy and so he refrained from leaving word for Luke. He swung north, entered the Sapphires, and rode up to the summer camp. The new men were getting along well, and the steers kept putting on weight. Satisfied, he came off the mountain and rode across to Eagle Point, afterward taking the notch to the bench.

He rode to the south end of the high mesa where, using field glasses, he took a look at the new fence. He could still make out the line of posts. There was no one in sight. He was gambling on Packwood's feeling his position was too shaky to defy the law openly just then. Yet he knew from bitter experience that Packwood, frustrated in one way, would lash out in another. His strikes were proving to be as vicious and deadly as a diamondback's.

CHAPTER THIRTEEN

Until they were at the edge of the hills, the violence at the shack still roaring in his head, Packwood bent himself to fast riding. At the moment he stood in awe of his foreman riding silently beside him, a man so easily rendered extreme and merciless. Hill shadow threw itself across the lane behind the long line fence. Packwood slowed then, his chest heaving from the hard travel.

'How'd you figure out where I was?' he said.

Hannegan slacked speed also. He looked at Packwood in twisted amusement. 'Pure luck. Thought I'd have to shoot my way into Mesa. So I stopped to get Finney. I caught onto the setup and got Reedy to help. What happened to Finney during all that fandango?'

Packwood threw up his hands. 'I don't know what made him do it. But he sold out to Mesa.'

'Why, the dirty devil. Well, we'll put a better man there.'

Packwood flung him a keyed-up glare. 'Not with Mesa holding a deed,' he said viciously. 'But we've got to get another man at Reedy Smith's and damned fast.'

'We will,' Hannegan said confidently. His glance traveled curiously over his boss's face. 'And in case you're feeling too good about this, I've got news. Your wife's lit her shack.

Vamoosed.'

Packwood stared at him in amazement. 'Have you gone clean crazy?'

Hannegan sent him a cutting regard, resenting the remark. His eyes danced in wicked relish. 'You won't think so when I tell you what she done. She's the one that stole the match case out of your desk. She took it to Mesa. I seen her go there from the mesa. I was pretty sure, and when I accused her she admitted it. I was scared to tell you, of what you'd do to her. She was scared I would, I guess, and lit out.' The foreman went on to relate what he had seen in the south hills that morning.

'Why didn't you stop her anyway?' Packwood said in a low, raging voice.

'I told you, she had a gun on me. She meant to use it.'

A killer's rage, like he had seen in Hannegan at Finney's shack, seized Packwood. Badly as he wanted to deny the truth of what he had heard, he could not. For a long while Abby had been withdrawn from him. More than once she had shown her distaste not only for his ways but for him as a man. He knew Atherton had disturbed her with what he said about the Tarrones that day on the road. So it was not unbelievable that she would betray him. Having done it once, she might go to the sheriff next with whatever she could tell him. This thought laced his outrage with fear that

157

grew equally cogent.

'She's still got to be stopped,' he said hoarsely. 'Get the men out. She'd be going to Las Vegas.'

'You want the boys to know what she's done?'

Packwood groaned. 'I guess not. You're a good tracker. Pick up her trail and catch her before she can get on a train. Bring her back.'

'She's had a good start,' Hannegan mused, 'but it's a long ways to Vegas, too.' The interruption over with, he could let his own thoughts return to her. He began to reflect Packwood's concern about her doing more damage still.

They rode thereafter in silence and soon reached Clover Leaf. Turning his lathered horse over to the foreman, Packwood went to his office and dropped exhaustedly to the chair at the desk. The note he had been forced to leave lay on the desk where Hannegan had dropped it. Packwood wadded and tossed it aside in disdain. Yet that triumph had already faded into his new worry. The tension and excitement had taken a good deal out of him. He pulled a bottle of whiskey out of his desk and took a stiff drink. He lighted a cigar.

Through the window he saw Hannegan walk from the corral to the cookshack for something to eat. A little later the foreman came angling across the yard to the office. His coolness infuriated Packwood. The man had

158

grown far too insolent. Yet in that moment Packwood realized his need of what Hannegan offered. He could spare his wife better than he could spare this man.

Hannegan said curtly, 'I'll be on my way. No saying when I'll be back.'

'Not just you—the two of you. Don't come back alone.'

'I guess you never found out what she's like,' Hannegan said musingly. 'She's not going to come back voluntarily. And if she gives me trouble I might have to get rough.'

After only a second's pause Packwood said, 'If you can't bring her back, see she can't go on.'

'You mean that?'

Packwood nodded. 'Do what you have to do, but don't let her get away.'

He felt no easier after he saw Hannegan pound out on the trail to the hills. It was galling that the ramrod should have been the first to learn that his wife was faithless. He grew more and more afraid of what she would do if she got away. A wife couldn't be forced to testify against her husband, but she could reveal plenty voluntarily. He knew now that Abby was ready to do anything against him. She could ruin him.

He put in a restless afternoon, his mind disorganized. The struggle in the basin became curiously remote and unreal for the time being. Hannegan couldn't make the ride to

Las Vegas and back under two or three days, which meant many hours of this torment.

Packwood forced himself to eat an evening meal, not wanting his men to suspect how he had had the insides cut out of him. He made himself go into the main house, long after dark, and encounter all the reminders of his traitorous wife. But he refused to sleep in the room they had shared. Instead he took a spare bed in the other end of the house.

He awakened out of feverish dreams in the first light. He found that something had settled and hardened in him. He remembered that Reedy Smith had been the price of his deliverance from Mesa's hands. He had to place another man on Smith's claim before Mesa grabbed it, he recalled. Shorty Halleck was the right type, a tough little turkey, cool in the pinches. Packwood washed, dressed, and went out to the yard.

To the puzzled men standing about he said, 'I had to send Hannegan to Vegas on some special business. You boys carry on with the work in the hills. Except you, Shorty. I want you to get over to Reedy's. and stay there. He was killed yesterday in a fracas Pierce and I had with Mesa.'

The men showed little surprise, and he supposed they had been putting two and two together. His shame at the defection of his wife seemed too hotly squirming in his mind not to be noticed and understood. The

160

punchers filed into the cookshack. Packwood had his own breakfast brought over to the office. Of course they knew Abby was gone and they probably guessed it had shaken Clover Leaf to its foundations.

About an hour later Shorty Halleck pulled up in front of the office in a raise of dust. He came bolting through the door and stared excitedly at Packwood.

'Boss,' he said in a voice cracked by excitement, 'they've fenced us off at the edge of the hills. Tore Reedy's out and moved it.'

Packwood looked at him with swelling eyes. 'Get my horse, Shorty,' he managed to say.

In ten minutes he was following the road that led down the hill bay to the basin. The short cowpuncher rode with him. Packwood soon saw the short low stripes of fence posts cutting from west to east where no fence had been before. The impact was as heavy as when Atherton so insolently subdued him in his own office. The fence had been erected in the night. As he rode up he saw that a gate had been left at the road—a mocking courtesy to Clover Leaf.

Packwood's anger ate at him like lye. His first desire was to gather his crew and undo this outrage. Yet a defeating thought rose to arrest it: that stroke of Atherton's in inducing Finney to sell out to him. Packwood knew he had no business tearing out the fence when he was already in a dangerous position over the killing of Tarrone. A new sensation would rock the country when word got out of Mike Terry's fate. There was the killing of Chase and Smith to be accounted for. Finally, Abby was bound to make more trouble if Hannegan failed to stop her.

'What're we gonna do about it?' Halleck said.

Packwood felt the will run out of him and he sighed. 'Nothing. You get on over to Reedy's.' An afterthought came, and he amended the order. 'Considering this step, they might have done something about that place, too. I'll go with you.'

Halleck opened the gate and let them through. Afterward they rode past the ex-Finney place. Packwood did not care to look that way and remember the violence and his ultimate defeat in it. They pressed on to Reedy Smith's. Packwood recognized instantly the old wagon standing in front of the house. When he rode up with Halleck the Tarrone girl appeared in the doorway with a rifle in her hands. The look in her eye gave Packwood pause.

'What're you doing here?' he said with a gasp.

'Living here. And we're not taking any lip from you about it, Packwood. You're a murdering devil. You fooled us a while about that but not long.'

Packwood's eyes closed for a second, a

162

sense of futility washing through him. Silently he cursed Hannegan's stupidity or brazenness in shooting so as to endanger Smith. That had been the result, he knew, of Hannegan's calculations. He had simply wanted to enhance his own safety in the delivery. It had resulted in this.

'You can't stay here,' he said roughly. 'Get out.'

'On whose say-so? Are you going into court and admit that Smith was your hireling here? That's what you'd have to do, Packwood, and it would get you trouble instead of us off of here.'

Once this fearlessly stubborn girl had pleased him and seemed useful. Now she spelled defeat. Nothing would persuade her to move off voluntarily. To get rough again would confess to having been rough when her father was killed. Without another word Packwood swung his horse and rode off with Halleck.

The time had come to strike the hardest, most conclusive blow he could manage against Mesa itself, and his fury made him yearn to strike it. He had never worried about the suspicion of guilt, only whether it could be proved. In this mood he allowed his inflamed mind free play when he reached Clover Leaf and shut himself in the office. Every fragment of his shattered pride called for revenge. Every impulse of greed demanded the total conquest of the Hueco.

163

His searching thoughts prodded at the herds of cattle belonging to his enemies and summering in the forests. Their loss would seal the doom of Mesa and Big Springs. Finally, Hannegan had told him about the extra cowhands Mesa had hired, seasoned hard cases out of God knew what background. The stroke he sought lay there somewhere. He had a feeling of its being on the edge of his mind, but there it stuck. He was still pacing the floor and chewing up cigars when night came. Hannegan might be back by another noon, with luck sooner, and he wanted his plans ready for action.

He was awake instantly when sometime in the early morning fast-hitting hoofs rapped in the ranchyard. Heaving himself from his bed, he slid to a window and looked out to see Hannegan's starlighted figure. He experienced a plummeting of hope. The man had returned from his chase alone.

He called, 'See you in the office, Pierce,' and hastily donned his trousers and boots.

Hannegan had lighted the office lamp when Packwood stepped in through the inside door. He was whiskery and gray with dust, and his eyes were hollow and burning.

'No luck, eh?' Packwood said dismally.

Hannegan eyed him coldly. 'Depends on how you look at it. I caught her short of Vegas. She wouldn't come back. She nearly got away from me. I had my orders in that case.'

164

'You—?'

'Put it this way. She won't give us any more trouble.'

It hit Packwood harder than he had expected. He had clung to the hope that Hannegan could induce or force her to return. But this was better than letting her get to the sheriff.

He had to take his mind off it, so he told the foreman about the Tarrones moving onto the Smith place. 'And I've made up my mind what your job will be. I want the Mesa and Big Springs cattle run out of the mountains. Maybe Atherton wasn't so smart hiring those gun-slinging drifters. Trusting them the way he has, anyhow. They could make the biggest rustling haul this country ever heard of, and he's giving them every chance to do it.'

'Them two in the Sapphires with the Mesa herd?' Hannegan said. His tired eyes had brightened with interest.

Packwood nodded. 'And the slim-jim Atherton's got with him at Mesa. Your first job is to latch onto those three rannies. Then you move off the cattle. Who's to say afterward that the three hard cases didn't do it?'

'That's a tall order,' Hannegan said.

'It's got to be tall. This is the showdown.'

Hannegan was silent while he put that through his mind. Packwood knew it was the kind of brash venture that would appeal to him strongly once he had thought it over. The foreman was himself eager to avenge the progress Atherton had made. He began to nod his shaggy head.

Smiling coolly now, Packwood said, 'If you were going to steal those herds yourself, how'd you go about it?'

'Well,' Hannegan said musingly, 'I sure couldn't beat the telegraph lines to the border. Even if I could fight off the chase that long. It'd have to be tricky and could be. A man could cross one of these damned deserts where the tracks would blow away in a few hours. He could stash the stuff in some secret valley and peddle it a little here and a little there.'

'Sure,' Packwood said. 'But we don't need to go that far. We'll only start on a plan that looks something like that. We'll get the cattle far enough on the desert they can't make it back alive. The new Mesa punchers have vanished. When the cattle are found, dead or dying, it will look like something scared them or they just gave it up as impossible and vamoosed.'

Hannegan laughed. 'You know, that's what's needed to explain old Terry, too. He got suspicious of those three strange rannies on Mesa. Maybe he caught them snooping and casing the thing and got done in so he couldn't spoil their game.'

'I thought of that. Now, make sure you've got them first. Then take care of the cattle. If you can get Atherton in the process so much the better. The rannies can be blamed for that, too. Now, get yourself some chuck and sleep a while. There's work to do.'

Hannegan was grinning when he went out.

Noticing that his hands had quit shaking as he lighted a cigar, Packwood sat in the yellow shine of the lamp. His world was settled again, and he felt his old naked power. It partly occurred to him that this was helped by Hannegan's being back on the ranch, but he checked the thought.

CHAPTER FOURTEEN

At the head of Mule Canyon the worn cow trail pitched onto a high plateau. The pack string topped out easily, Rip driving it, bringing his first load of salt out to the range. The boy needed no help, Pick noticed all the way from Mesa. He rode a horse like he had been born on its back. Even the pack animals responded to him naturally. They had left Mesa right after breakfast, and it was around ten when they reached the plateau.

Having emerged from the canyon, Pick rode up beside Rip and said, 'You're doing all right. You must have done some packing before.'

Rip shook his head. 'I just like horses. And cows, too.'

'You'll get plenty of both at roundup.'

Rip looked at him quickly, his eyes gleaming. 'You'll let me ride with the outfit? I mean really work with it?'

'Can't keep you rousting forever.'

Rip put that through his mind. He looked at Pick questioningly. 'Look, is it because of Piper? I mean—you got your eye on her or something? I don't want you helping me because of anything like that.'

'A man couldn't be blamed for noticing her,' Pick said. 'She's a mighty attractive girl. But mainly you're a good hand, and I need good

168

hands.' He found that he really meant that. Rip was no deadhead.

The string traveled steadily along the slope, angling toward the summer camp, which it reached in another ten minutes. The camp was deserted, the cook fire cold. 'You unload the salt,' Pick said, 'and I'll hunt up the boys.'

He rode on over the plateau. Everywhere he looked he could see Mesa cattle grazing peacefully. But the new men, Hammond and Parker, were not in sight. He went on to Lone Tree Spring, then over to where a stream ran a short distance across the range and disappeared underground. He still saw nothing of the cowhands.

He was turning back toward camp, puzzled, when it came. The crash of a rifle rent the silent morning.

The bullet came so close he knew he was in mortal danger. He raked his spurs along the horse's ribs, sending it streaking for the closest cover, a rock pile a hundred feet to his right. The rifle rapped again and yet again before he made it. Each time he knew he'd had a close brush with death.

Swung in behind a looming boulder, he looked about, his eyes bright with anger. The source of the shooting was another rock crop ahead on his previous line of travel. He hadn't looked for anything like this to happen or he would have been wary of that spot. He jerked up his gun although it was next to useless at that distance.

He sat there trembling in his eagerness to get on top of this, to understand it. It dawned on him that he and the other man were both pinned down. The ground beyond the far rockery climbed, and the attacker could not cross it without being seen. Pick couldn't retreat without coming into view again within gun range. Neither of them could cross the space toward each other except in a highly reckless rush. The other man had intended to kill him, and now they were deadlocked.

He wondered if Rip could have heard the shots at the camp. But the boy wasn't armed even if he had heard and understood. He began to feel sweat leak down his sides, a hot impatience crowding him. There had to be a Clover Leaf man over there, and he wanted to nail him.

All at once hoofs beat the earth hard and fast. A horse and rider went streaking out due away from him. The rider was beyond pistol range already. He had used that fact to break the deadlock. But that was only a stray thought in Pick's mind as he stared in shocked discernment. He knew the horse. It was the one Bede Hammond had ridden when he reported for work at Mesa. There was no telling if Bede was the man on its back, for the rider had flattened himself and was faced in the other direction. Man and mount vanished swiftly into the far timber, leaving him utterly mystified and profoundly worried.

He reholstered his useless pistol, his mouth hard-ruled and grim. He swung about and headed for the cow camp at a rush.

In a matter of minutes he saw Rip break into view, streaking toward him. Some of the hardness left Pick's eyes. Rip had heard the shots, all right. Being unarmed hadn't frightened him out of riding up to help. The kid had what it took and a little over.

'What happened?' Rip called as they closed the gap.

'You've got me, Rip,' Pick said. 'Somebody threw some shots at me. He was riding that whitestocking bay of Bede Hammond's.'

'Bede?' Rip said with a gasp. 'He tried to shoot you?'

'All I know is that it was his horse.'

'What does it mean? Have they gone over to Clover Leaf?'

'That's what I wonder, Rip.' He didn't know the two men up here as well as he had come to know Hosea. It was not impossible that they had sold out to Packwood and set a trap to kill him.

He rode on with Rip to the camp and finished unloading the salt. One thing was certain: the cattle had been left unattended. So he had to get Pecos and Hosea up here immediately, although pulling everyone out of the basin might be part of the plan under way. Rip would have to return to Mesa alone. He

171

explained the situation, and Rip was ready to do it.

They hobbled the pack string and turned it on the grass so the boy wouldn't be encumbered with it. 'You rode with the boys enough to know where to find them,' Pick said. 'Tell them to drop everything and get up here.'

'You think Bede and Corb turned rustlers?'

'I don't know what to think, Rip. Get riding.'

Rip was gone like a shot. Pick rode back to where he could see most of the scattered cattle. Disdaining the continuing danger, he began to ride a loose circle about the steers. It wasn't inconceivable that the stray riders had decided it was too good a rustling setup to pass by. But he wasn't swallowing that any more than the idea that Clover Leaf had hired them to kill him. He reached the end of the plateau and swung back on the lower side. He wasn't molested again.

His unexpected arrival might have broken up the mysterious play for the time being, but he couldn't bank on it. He set to work bunching the cattle tighter. The thought of Clover Leaf combined in his mind with the rustling explanation and made more sense than either separately. Packwood would profit more than rustlers if something happened to these steers. He hoped the sheriff reached the basin soon. He could, for Pecos had got back from the telegraph office the day before.

Satisfied that none of the steers were where they could be moved into the timber easily, Pick found the trail of the man who shot at him. He had a brightly angry determination to settle that particular question. He began to follow the sign along the plateau. Presently he came to where it disappeared into the head of a canyon that dropped on the desert side of the mountain. Recklessness impelled him to persist and go on. Yet wisdom counseled waiting until he had help so as not to leave the steers unguarded. He turned back reluctantly.

The sun stood high and burning over the ranges by then. Having returned to the camp, he started a fire, got fresh water from the spring, and made a pot of coffee. There were red beans in the kettle. When they were warm he filled a tin plate and ate a meal. He filled a coffee cup and sat on his heels while he smoked a cigarette.

His thoughts were bleakly stubborn. Four men had died in the struggle for the basin. That warned that from there on the sky was the limit as far as Clover Leaf was concerned. He measured that and accepted it. He knew that when the dust settled again either Mesa or Clover Leaf would be destroyed.

He saw a man bob out of the canyon on the basin side and sprang to his feet. The scrawny, stiff-gaited nag soon told him the rider was Sam. The old prospector poked across the plateau. When he came up his face was set in hard lines. He slid off the horse, came over to the fire, and wordlessly filled a tin cup.

'Have some beans,' Pick said, wondering what had brought him.

Sam shook his head, took a swig of coffee, and wiped a hand across his mouth.

'Run into Rip. He told me you lost a couple of your new hands.'

'That's right, and I sure don't know how come.'

'They ain't been night-herding, have they?'

Pick shook his head. 'Didn't seem to be any reason up here.'

'Then it would be easy for somebody to come up on them in their beds and throw down on them.'

Pick's eyes narrowed. 'Think they're being held prisoner, Sam?'

'That or they're dead, like Mike and Tarrone.'

Pick nodded. 'Well, that's been in the back of my mind, I guess. But it don't make much sense.'

'Everything makes sense when you understand it. I knew you were shorthanded. Figured I'd come up and help.'

'I'm sure glad you did. If you want to ride herd on the stuff, I'd like to scout the timber.'

'Go ahead.'

Pick soon cut the sign that had interested him previously. He followed it back to the north-side canyon. He entered the stricture at

174

once, the feeling strong in him that there was a much more elaborate action under way here than seemed apparent on the surface. The canyon shadows fell across him and burnt lava rock bulged out of the walls. The man he followed had been going fast when he came down through here. The hoofprints occasionally visible were cut deeply, with loose dirt thrown out.

The canyon soon broke into another, smaller meadow. Before he emerged Pick reined in and took a good look at the prospect before him. A breeze fanned the grass and sage, and the distant timber lay in a wash of light. He rode farther out and with a look to the right saw something that made him pull back hastily.

Dismounting, he dropped the reins and moved forward on foot, keeping the brushy foot slope covering him. He knew there was a spring up there ahead. Just for a moment he had thought he saw something moving through the thin screen of nut pine about it.

He climbed a short way on the slope, his gun in his hand. In the mixture of gravel and detritus he had to place each step with care. He made his way slowly forward, watching carefully. All at once he saw a temporary camp in the stand of pine. Bede Hammond and Corb Parker were sitting there stolidly. Pick's eyes glinted as he stopped, considering the situation.

In a moment he angled higher on the rise and crept on, then began to slip down directly above the camp. Presently he could see into the camp again. Now he was positioned so he could see a Clover Leaf puncher cut from sight before. It was Skip Gorman, who sat with his back to a rock and a carbine across his lap. It was impossible to tell whether Hammond and Parker were there voluntarily or were being held there by Gorman.

Pick frowned. If the two Mesa punchers were prisoners he might get them shot by acting rashly. He was within pistol range but from his position would have a poor chance at Gorman. He studied the ground below and decided to move farther south. If Hammond and Parker had defected to the enemy he wanted to settle it with them. If they had been captured by Clover Leaf they were already in mortal danger.

Pick started to turn and move again when a voice drilled through the wild silence.

'Lose something, Atherton?'

Pick flung a startled glance up the slope. Shorty Halleck stood there with a six-gun leveled on him, thinly smiling.

'Had a feeling you'd poke down this way,' Halleck said. 'Keep your hands away from that shooting iron.' He came down the slope. 'A cuss as reckless as you ought to have the brains to go with it, Atherton. We figured one of us had better keep stashed out. Drop that gun

176

belt and walk away from it.'

Pick stood motionless, strongly goaded to defiance. The deadliness of Halleck's eyes told him he would be killed promptly if he resisted. He unbuckled his gun belt and let the rig fall, then took a few steps away. Halleck slid in and swept up the weapon.

'Now you can come and satisfy your curiosity,' he said.

Pick moved downward toward the camp at the spring, Halleck following. He saw surprise leap onto the faces of Bede and Corb. Gorman showed the same reaction, but he was the only one pleased by it. Pick saw that the Mesa riders had also been disarmed. Deadly as the situation was, he was relieved that they had not betrayed him.

'Good work, Shorty,' Gorman said in high confidence. 'Your idea of hiding out sure filled our bobtail flush.'

The Mesa men showed the effect of long tension, so they had been here a while. Neither said anything except with their eyes, which spoke eloquently. Sam had guessed it right, he decided. They had been surprised and overcome in camp. Halleck must have been the one on Bede's horse, laying in wait for him. He had used that horse to confuse the issue in case the waylay failed.

Halleck motioned Pick over beside the other prisoners and took a look at the sun. 'Time Pierce and Eddie got here with the slim-jim,' he said. 'I wish to hell they'd hurry.'

'We got three of them,' Gorman said. 'What's the use of riding herd on them when we don't need to?' He fondled the gun.

'Pierce said to have them all, first. But he'd better get here. We've got a lot left to do.'

'It's wholesale murder this time, is it?' Pick said bitterly. He was looking at the runty Halleck. 'Then a wholesale rustling job, I take it, to throw the whole basin to Clover Leaf.'

Bede said disgustedly, 'They've got it figured out, Pick. Gorman's like a lot of men who're only as big as their gun. Me and Corb and Hosea are to be blamed for it. Strangers you shouldn't have trusted taking advantage of the situation. We're to be hidden where we won't be found. You're to be found, shot by the rustlers, naturally. They figure to clean out Big Springs, too. Gorman got bored setting here. He bragged about it.'

'You want the butt end of this in your teeth?' Gorman said, lifting the carbine. He was angered by the gibe, not by what Bede had revealed.

'It'll take more than brags,' Pick said to Gorman. 'How do you expect to get away with so much stuff?'

'That's our worry.'

'You'd better worry. I sent for the sheriff day before yesterday. You're apt to run into him with hot cattle on your hands.'

Halleck cut in to say sharply, 'Sheriff? What

for?'

'Hannegan killed Blackie Chase and Reedy Smith. Or didn't you boys know that?'

Halleck exchanged a quick look with Gorman.

Pressing it, Pick said, 'I wouldn't go out on a limb for Packwood and Hannegan. There's a reason why they threw everything into the pot. You with it, half blind to what the situation really is. You'd better turn us loose and not stick your necks in a noose they haven't let you see.'

Gruffly Gorman said, 'He's bluffing, Shorty. Anyhow, it don't matter about the sheriff. We don't have far to go with them steers. Just lose 'em on the desert.'

Halleck nodded. Pick realized he wasn't going to rattle them enough to help. All he could do was stall the showdown as long as he could. Sam might get suspicious when he failed to return to the herd. The old prospector could get around in these ranges like a Piute. It hadn't occurred to the Clover Leaf hands that he was anywhere near.

CHAPTER FIFTEEN

Luke had told her flatly to quit riding alone and to stay close to the house at all times. But Olive could no longer stand being cooped up by herself day after dragging day. He was gone from morning to night, refusing her help with the work, although Mike's death had increased it enormously for him. When he did come home he only said what he was forced to say to her and that in a cold, curt way. His censure had spread to other things now. He resented everything she was, had ever been, or could ever be.

He had left the house after an early breakfast, red-eyed and worn out. Rebelling, Olive had saddled her horse and ridden out. Yet she had respected his wishes in one thing. She had not poked off into the dangerous Piutes. Instead she had ridden here to Skillet Springs, under the Sapphires. That was about as far away from Clover Leaf as she could get without leaving the basin. She had loosened the cinch and let her horse graze while she stretched out by the spring, the old cottonwoods shading her. She was trying to muster the courage to slip away from Big Spring forever but could not make the decision.

She didn't realize she was drowsy, having

180

slept but little in the night, until her eyes came open with a start. Fast-driving hoofs beat the earth somewhere close. She felt their vibration in the ground more than she heard them. She lifted her head and stared outward. For a second her grogginess kept her eyes out of focus. Then they sharpened on the outer distance.

Riders were coming in a hard drive across the flat, three of them. She realized they were aiming for these springs. She sprang to her feet, her heart running in a ragged rhythm. Catching the bridle reins, she led the horse deeper into the brush. Her knees seemed to have no strength in them.

Until she knew who it was she could only hide there, for she couldn't mount and strike for home unseen. Luke's warning came back to her with impact. She stood at the horse's head, concealed by the brush, hoping she could keep the animal from betraying her.

The men drew up at the springs. Her weak knees nearly buckled when she recognized Hannegan and another Clover Leaf man, Grachell. Then she realized that the tall, lean rider with them was the new man Pick had hired, the one they called Hosea.

Hannegan and Grachell swung down. Hannegan looked up at Hosea and said roughly, 'Get down if you want to wet your whistle. But if you try anything you're dead.'

The words stabbed through Olive like

181

hurled knives. She stood in sick dread that someone would look her way. All at once one of them did, but it was Hosea. She feared he would give some sign, but his self-control was excellent. For a second some kind of plea showed in his eyes. Or maybe she put it there by knowing he hoped this was a break, that somehow she could help him. Then he looked away quickly.

'Take it I'm gonna die anyhow,' he said in a drawl. 'Like the man you just killed—Pecos Benton. How do you expect to get away with all this murder, Hannegan?' Olive realized he was talking so as to convey as much information to her as he could. He wanted her help desperately, and she was helpless herself.

'You're the one who killed Pecos,' Hannegan said easily. 'Just like you're going to kill Atherton. I told you the day I met you coming in that you were picking the wrong side in this business. You want a drink or not?'

'The hell with your water,' Hosea said. 'Let's get on to your Sapphire hideout and get it over with.' Sapphire hideout—that was more information Hosea wanted her to have.

'Watch him, Eddie,' Hannegan said, and dropped down to drink at the spring.

He, in turn, guarded the prisoner while the other man quenched his thirst. Then the Clover Leaf men swung up, and the three went on across the flat. Olive's eyes closed, and the world turned black for a second. She had to risk moving out farther to see where they went. They were bearing on the nearby canyon into the Sapphires, toward Clover Leaf's hideout, of course.

She stood in panic, with no idea what she could do. Another man had been killed, apparently Pecos, while they took Hosea into their hands. Such a rampage meant that Clover Leaf was out to end the resistance against it. She thought of Luke, but it would take hours to reach him, and she had to know where in the Sapphires they took Hosea. She hadn't even a gun, yet she began at once to tighten the latigo of her saddle.

When she turned to look again the riders had vanished into the purple mouth of the canyon. She stepped up to the saddle, her jaw firming. In her first failure she hadn't realized the seriousness of the situation. Now she was all too clear on it. She rode out of the brush and toward the canyon. She had never been on that mountain, and it was like riding into perdition itself.

The stricture swallowed her and was so narrow and twisting she saw no one ahead. As long as its walls remained solid all she had to do was follow behind, staying far enough back to escape notice. If they caught her they would be obliged to kill her, too, for she now carried deadly information about them. She accepted that and fought down the sickness it raised in her.

She knew the canyon pointed north. The sun fell into it fully from behind, so she had slept longer than she had realized. The going was slow and difficult, and presently she began to feel a pain in her side. It reminded her that the doctor had told her to quit riding until after the baby was born. A fear stabbed through her but only that she wouldn't be able to keep on. It was a stitch, probably, from the jolting and swaying.

For a long while she moved quietly behind the three men. Then the canyon headed in a high meadow, increasing her problem. She came onto the open ground and reined in, puzzled. After a moment she detected the men, moving against the far timber. She waited and watched until they had vanished into the timber then she followed.

When she came to the other side of the meadow she grew panicky, no longer able to distinguish the point where they had vanished into the trees. It occurred to her tardily that she should have followed their tracks instead of cutting straight across the open. There were no tracks in evidence where she reined in, and she sat in perplexity. Maybe they had traveled farther out from the timber than she had thought. Maybe she had pointed too far to the right.

After a moment she swung the horse and rode to the left. Relief broke through her when she found the place where they had turned into the woods. She followed through the open trees, her eyes glued to the sign now. The pain really beat in her side by then. She stuck to the tracks, and presently they dropped over into another canyon. She wondered how much farther they would take Hosea, how long it would be before they stopped. When they did she would be confronted with the total impossibility of the thing she had to accomplish.

This canyon was short, ending so abruptly it gave her a scare. She halted inside to see, falling away ahead of her, a meadow like the one behind. She had no idea where they were by then or how she would get home if she lived to do it. She ventured out into the open, only to pull back at once.

Down along the edge of the mountain a patch of nut pine ran out a distance, and in it she could see several dismounted men and their mounts. Hannegan and his companions were halting there, two of them swinging down. She had a feeling of having been hit hard under the breastbone, and her lungs seemed paralyzed. There was nothing she could do, now that she had followed them here.

Yet she dismounted and walked forward, her muscles impelling action even when her mind could reach no decision. Rocks sheltered her at the canyon mouth, and she moved in closer to the Clover Leaf rendezvous. She saw

Hosea get off his horse presently and noticed another tall man standing there. It dawned on her that this was Pick, a prisoner, too. Hannegan's words at the springs rang in her ears. She alone stood between helpless men and a merciless death, and there was nothing at all she could do.

The realization that there was something came like a piece of ice sliding into her mind, needling and chilling her. She turned and crept back to her horse. Swinging into the saddle, she rode out into full view.

She sat there trembling, waiting for them to see her. At last she saw a man stiffen and stare her way. He pointed and said something excitedly. The others turned to look toward her. Sure that they knew of her presence, that there was someone who could tell on them, she whipped her horse into the canyon and sent it driving up the grade.

She could never escape, yet the confusion she had created might give the Mesa men their chance. She urged the horse onward, praying it could keep its feet on the rough trail. After a few minutes she reined in, listening intently. She heard hoofs drum the earth behind. Again she plunged on through the climbing canyon.

*　　　*　　　*

Rip rode like the wind after he left the Mesa camp, feeling the enormous responsibility Pick had entrusted to him. In recent days his feeling for the tall man had changed vastly. What at first had been a bitter hatred like Piper's was now something like he had once felt for Kit Carson or Buffalo Bill. Only a Clover Leaf bullet could have stopped him as he sent his horse driving down the canyon to the basin. It might even take hours to run Pecos and Hosea down, and there was no telling what would happen in the forest before he got up there with them.

The first thing the two punchers did each morning of late was to check to see how Ma and Piper were making out. Rip had appreciated that deeply, knowing it was to ease his worry about them. Then they rode on to Gap Springs. After that they checked the new fence Mesa had thrown across the Clover Leaf bay, then they angled over to the springs south of the mesa. He figured he would try to intercept them at the south end of the playa. If he got there too late he could follow until he caught up. That failing, God forbid, he would have to wait and catch them at headquarters when they went in at noon to eat.

It took a while just to reach the extending flat and cross it to the upper end of the playa. That brought him so close to home Rip swung over, although Pecos and Hosea would have passed there. Piper, dressed in overalls and shirt, was repairing the corral fences Reedy Smith had let run down badly. She had all kinds of plans in her head, as he did, about building up the cattle they would run for Mesa until they had a herd of their own.

When she saw the way he whipped in, Piper straightened, looking at him intently. He saw fear strike through her as she started toward him.

'What's wrong, Rip?' she called forward.

'Pecos and Hosea been by here yet this morning?'

Piper nodded. 'Quite a while ago. What's up?'

'There's been shooting at the herd. Pick wants them there.'

He saw her eyes close and was aware that something in her had changed greatly, too. This was not the sullen, touchy girl he had known so much of the time when their father was alive and they were traipsing around the country. She spoke quietly.

'Is Pick all right?'

It wasn't the first time he had noticed her thoughts were mightily on the man she once had wanted to kill. He wondered whether there was any chance she and Pick would get sweet enough to marry. It could happen. This quick fear of Piper's about Pick matched the way he'd seen Pick look at her after they quit fighting. Not in the hot greedy way he'd seen men look at her along the trail, but sort of yearning. A wanting look that wasn't offensive but clean and all right with Rip.

'Don't worry about Pick,' he said. 'He can take care of himself.'

'What was the shooting about?'

'Those sidekicks of Hosea's just faded into thin air and somebody tried to shoot Pick. Maybe they're trying to rustle or it's another job of Clover Leaf's.'

'Clover Leaf,' she said bitterly. 'Well, you'd better find the others.'

Rip agreed. He rode by the door, called a greeting to his mother, then went on toward Gap Springs.

They weren't there or at the line fence. Rip cut back sharply, heading toward the mesa behind headquarters. The position of the sun told him precious time was passing. He would check the rim ahead, then go over the top, and drop down to the house. If they weren't there yet he would try to head them on their regular circuit.

As he neared the spring at the foot of the rimrock he saw a horse standing there saddled. It looked like the boys were taking a rest, and Rip hurried on. A little later he frowned. There was only the one horse grazing. Its reins were up on its neck like somebody had gone out of the saddle without intending. He raked his spurs and came up to the horse, catching its check strap, then leaning down to get hold of the reins. Leading the animal, he rode on to the spring. All at once, his heart contracted, and he nearly went out of the saddle himself.

Pecos lay there on the ground. Blood had run out from under him, soaking the soil. He was badly hurt or dead.

Rip sprang from the saddle and sprinted forward. The horror of his life came when he saw that Pecos had been shot through the heart and killed instantly. Rip's wild look about showed him nothing of what had happened to Hosea. Suspicion seared through his mind. Had Hosea killed Pecos treacherously to get away and help steal the cattle? Somehow he couldn't believe it. Something else had happened here.

He found indications in a moment, plenty of them. Two horses had been hidden in the brush beyond the springs. They had waited quite a while, for there were droppings and lots of tracks, then they had moved out. When he followed the tracks, Rip saw they joined those of a third horse.

His mind quickly pictured a pair of Clover Leaf men. He had his choice of guessing whether, after ambushing Pecos, they had taken Hosea prisoner or he had joined them voluntarily. Again he could only give the tall thin man the benefit of doubt. He'd bet Pecos had been killed without warning, with Hosea covered so he had no chance to resist. Or both had been covered, then Pecos killed because Hosea was the one they wanted.

Rip's shocked thoughts came swiftly to the question of what he should do. He refused to leave Pecos in the hot sun like a dead animal. He caught a horse and managed to get him onto the saddle. He tied him securely enough to ride, then headed across the flat. Piper could take care of this. He had to get back and warn Pick that the enemy was on the move everywhere.

He knew Piper almost fainted when he came into the yard again, leading a horse with a dead man. He told her in tight, tumbling words what he had experienced.

'I've got to tell Pick,' he said finally. 'You'll have to take care of Pecos.'

She caught the reins of the led horse and waved Rip on.

He was plunging through the notch under Eagle Point when he again picked up sign. Three horses had come through there and hit off at an angle toward Skillet Springs. It couldn't have been long ago. It came to him that he might be able to overtake them and help Hosea some way. He ought to try that instead of taking time to go up to the Mesa camp first. The thought alone put a knot in his stomach, but he lined out, streaking for Skillet Springs.

He found where they had watered and then had struck off toward the secondary canyon leading into the Sapphires. He followed without hesitation, still crowding his horse. The canyon slowed him, for it was rougher than the main one to the summer range. He grew aware that a fourth horse had gone along here behind the first three, and that puzzled him even more.

He was glad of the kid years when he and Piper practiced rangecraft, often trailing wanted men of their own invention. That helped him when he topped out of the canyon into a high meadow he had never seen before. He had just entered it, carefully tracking, when a horse broke out of the far timber, driving toward him. He whipped back into cover, earnestly wishing he had a gun. Then he saw the streaming hair that told him the oncomer was a woman. Apparently she hadn't seen him for she came straight on.

As she neared he realized she was Luke Gallatin's wife, whom he had once seen at a distance. He rode out, waving his hat over his head, hoping she knew that meant he was friendly. Apparently she did, for she came on toward him.

As she drew up she said in a panting way, 'Oh—you don't have a gun.'

'Who's chasing you, ma'am?' Rip said tightly.

'Clover Leaf. They—'

He had learned enough and wondered if she realized how badly her horse was spent from the hard riding in the far canyon. He swung out of the saddle and said quietly, 'Get aboard my horse, ma'am, and light out for home. I'll try and throw them off your trail.'

'They'd kill you, too.'

'They ain't chasing me, ma'am. Do what I tell you.'

She glanced desperately backward, hesitated, then stepped down, and mounted his horse. 'I hadn't ought—' she began, but he slapped the horse and sent it off toward the south canyon.

He mounted hers. She had barely vanished when three riders broke one after the other from the north timber. Then he went driving along the other edge of the meadow, bent low. That made it hard to tell that the horse they followed had a new rider. It turned them after him.

His heart was beating as fast as the hoofs of the horse. He doubted that he would be dealt with gently if they caught him. But he had drawn them away from the woman. His one chance now was to make it over the ridge to the Mesa camp, where Pick could help him. He hoped this winded horse could keep going.

CHAPTER SIXTEEN

The riders came out of the grass-grown canyon across from the one by which he had ridden into the deadfall. Pick saw in bleak certainty that one of the new arrivals was Hosea. His glance shuttled to meet Bede's and an explosive satisfaction came out of Gorman.

'They got the slim-jim, Shorty,' Gorman said with gusto.

Halleck nodded, a quieter pleasure streaking his inset eyes. 'This seems to be our day, all right.' It was the most pleasant remark he had made so far.

The approaching trio rode in across the meadow. Hannegan raked his inspection over the Mesa riders, nodding in satisfaction. Pick was all too aware of the wild excitement in the man's eyes, a bright ferocity that was animal in its impact. Hannegan expected to smell blood or had smelled it already. The intoxication of it had him.

'She's ready to roll, Pierce,' Gorman said, 'and I'm damned tired of this setting still. Let's start our rustlers' war.'

Hannegan's brittle look shut him up. The Clover Leaf foreman swung down with Grachell. Pick waited for the rattle-mouthed Gorman to mention that the sheriff was on his way to the basin. He doubted that it would stop Hannegan even if he believed it. Clover Leaf had gone so far now it could only go ahead. The ramrod motioned Hosea to get down, and Hosea swung out of the leather. The gangling puncher's eyes, Pick noticed, were hard as the points of rock drills.

'They killed Pecos,' Hosea told him quietly. 'Shot him from hiding and had me covered before I knew what was up. Real sporting, ain't they?'

Pick got to his feet in a surge of rebellion, but Gorman's raspy voice sang out. 'Stop right there, buck, or you'll get a slug in your belly.'

Pick froze. Hannegan looked at the sun, thought a moment, and said, 'Since you're itching to pull a trigger, Gorman, you can take care of these strangers. You know where to hide their carcasses. We want Atherton killed where he's to be found.' The brutal order was delivered as casually as if Hannegan had been ticking off the daywork.

Then Grachell's voice ripped out. 'Who the hell's that up there?'

He pointed excitedly to the canyon by which Hannegan's party had come onto the high meadow. They all swung to stare through the growing heat. Pick saw the mounted figure up there. He recognized the Big Springs horse and detected that the rider was a woman. Olive? It hardly seemed possible. Yet he heard a gasp of satisfaction from Hosea.

'That sweet, nervy girl,' the thin man said. 'I

195

was afraid she never had the courage.'

Hannegan roared, 'Get her. You stay here, Gorman. Kill them all now if you have to.'

Pick watched desperately for a chance to make use of the confusion Olive had provided at such risk to herself. But Gorman had sprung to his feet, the carbine ready to drop anybody who moved menacingly. Hannegan, Halleck, and Grachell ran to their horses and sprang up. In a moment they were driving across the meadow, although the figure that drew them had vanished. Pick looked back to study Gorman, who obviously was uneasy at being alone with the prisoners.

A wild rebellion strained Pick's caution to the breaking point. He didn't understand what had brought Olive up here, but her chance of getting away again was next to none.

Looking on past Gorman, he let his voice fall across the silence. 'Shoot him, Sam. Don't give the snake a chance.'

Gorman couldn't help himself. He swung to look up the empty slope behind him. He swung back wildly, but by then Pick was driving at him. The other Mesa riders surged in, rattling Gorman further. He managed to trigger one shot. Pick felt the heat of the bullet on his cheek as he closed the gap. He brought Gorman down. The others piled on, spread-eagling the Clover Leaf puncher. When Pick sprang to his feet he had the carbine.

'Tie him to a tree,' he said gustily. 'My horse

is in the west canyon. A couple of you will have to ride double, but get out of here fast.'

He found his gun but was also carrying the carbine when he swung onto the nearest saddled horse. He went driving across the open toward the south canyon.

Its walls soon swallowed him, and the climb was broken and steep. He knew the others yearned to be in on the chase, but there were only two more horses there. Their only weapon was the pistol Gorman wore. But it was enough at the moment that they were out of the deathtrap. They would lose no time getting themselves out of Clover Leaf's reach until they were equipped to fight it out.

He came out of the canyon into the other meadow. He knew it, that the drop-down canyon lay straight across. He cut directly over instead of following the course the others had taken along the edge of the timber. His opinion of Olive had shot up a mile. She had found a shrewd way to break up a situation she could not dominate. She had been ready to throw her life away to do it. He wondered what had transpired, for Hosea seemed not to have been surprised by her action.

The chase was probably ten minutes ahead of him. He would need luck to be sure which way they had gone from this point. He reached the south canyon and entered it without slacking speed. But he had gone only a short distance when he realized that, while several horses had come in from the opposite direction recently, there was only one set of tracks going down. Clover Leaf must be trying to get ahead by some other route and cut Olive off.

The only thing to do was press as hard as he could, hoping to gain enough distance to be on hand if they tried to do anything to her. He put the horse on down at breakneck speed. Its shoes now and then struck sparks from the rocks. The rider ahead had ridden at an equal gait, he could tell by the tracks. If it was Olive she was a first-rate horsewoman.

It seemed a long while before he broke out on the open lower slope of the Sapphires. Rushing on to a high point, he took a scanning look at the country below him. He could see Skillet Springs and on across to the cottonwood patch at Big Springs. Just short of the far timber a rider was going like the devil chased him, and it must be Olive.

He sat in stiff-cheeked wonder as to what had happened to the Clover Leaf bunch. It seemed impossible that Hannegan would let her go carrying information that could hang them. More trickery was involved, likely. He knew he had better go on and make sure she was safe.

He reached Big Springs to find Olive armed with a rifle and waiting for him.

'You,' she said in enormous relief. 'You did get away.'

'Thanks to you, Olive,' Pick said, panting from the hard riding. 'What put you wise to it?'

She told him in words as breathless as his own.

'Good for Rip,' he said grimly. 'He likely made it for our camp, but Sam wasn't carrying a gun, either. I've got to get up there. You're safe for the time being, but go and find Luke.'

'I will.'

'I'd better rope fresh horses.'

'You'll have to have one, but don't waste time on me. I can get one for myself.'

'Take the rifle.'

She nodded and he rode out. Fifteen minutes later he was freshly mounted and cutting across the flat toward the main canyon to the summer camp. He hadn't wanted to alarm Olive, but the prospects of Rip and Sam escaping Clover Leaf vengeance were slim.

He was about to enter the main canyon when, slacking speed, he heard the rush of massed hoofs above him. Pulling back into the brush, he waited, the carbine at ready. In a moment three men spilled out of the canyon, Hannegan and the two punchers he had taken with him.

Pick lifted the carbine to his shoulder, on the point of opening up on them, then he reconsidered. They cut off in the other direction. He realized they were driving for Clover Leaf to pick up more men for a big scale man hunt in the Sapphires. Either they had taken care of Rip and Sam or something had turned them away from them.

He waited to be sure they were going to Clover Leaf and not Big Spring. Then he entered the canyon and began climbing swiftly. Luke would realize the danger to Olive and keep her out of their hands. Hannegan would have other men trying to hunt down the unarmed contingent from Mesa. Pick topped the grade, ran across the plateau, and came up to the camp. It was deserted.

He was only a little relieved that there were no bodies there. For several minutes he sat his saddle, catching his breath and considering. Then several men rode out of the timber to his right. One of them waved his hat. Pick let out a gusty sigh as they drew nearer. He detected Sam and Rip and the others. They rode in grimly.

'How'd you manage to shake them, boy?' Pick asked Rip.

Sam explained it. When considerable time had expired without Pick's coming back he began to realize something had gone wrong. He had mounted his horse to follow, when a rider came charging out of the timber, others not far behind him. Thinking it was Pick being pursued by Clover Leaf, Sam had grabbed the iron rod over the cold fire. Holding it so it looked like a rifle barrel, he had driven straight at them. It had turned Clover Leaf off.

'Hannegan went after more men,' Pick said. 'Then they'll comb the hills for us and Olive. The first thing's to get armed, then we'd better team up with Luke and Olive. Their plan of rustling and making it look like the reason for killing me is shot. They'll give that up, so we don't need to worry about the herd.'

'Just ourselves,' Bede said bitingly. 'They've gone so far they can't leave us alive.'

They moved down off the mountain and reached Mesa headquarters in the middle of the afternoon. Once the men were re-armed a new mood settled on them. Pick sent them on to Big Springs, saying he would join them later. He headed for Piper's place. He knew she would be mightily concerned for Rip. The dead man left in her care had to be buried.

She was worried, her mother sharing the tension. Both of them hurried out when they saw Pick riding in. He told them what had taken place.

'Clover Leaf rode by here,' Piper said. 'But they didn't even look our way.'

'They've got enough on their hands. The sheriff could show any time, Piper. I want you to keep a lookout and warn him of what's going on. In their desperation they'd kill him if they had to.'

The frightened way Piper looked at him made his heart turn over. He knew she wasn't thinking of herself. The change in this girl was more apparent in that moment than it had ever been before. With the defensiveness gone a woman's natural gentleness lay exposed. He wondered if the pendulum could have swung to its opposite, her hatred of him becoming something precious and wonderful.

She kept meeting his eyes as if she knew the question in his mind and was ready to give her answer.

Gently he said, 'Rip proved himself two hundred per cent a man up there, Piper. I know he's got a sister who's that much woman.' Maybe it wasn't a pretty compliment, but it came from the depths of his heart.

'Thank you, Pick.'

She insisted on helping him in the bitter task of burying Pecos. When she tipped her head for a simple prayer Pick pulled off his hat, and in that moment, standing man and woman in tragedy, they passed beyond all doubt of what was to be between them.

The depression and aftermath of violence were gone when Pick rode out. They had broken the back of Clover Leaf's big and final move. Even though it left them confronted by a more desperate enemy it was a substantial gain.

The Gallatins had forted up at Big Springs, where they had been joined by Pick's friends. One look at Olive showed Pick that the haunting unhappiness was gone. Luke also seemed different. The well-armed aggregation had given them all a new spirit, and the housewife in Olive had asserted itself. She was cooking a meal for the men, who had not eaten in a great while. Luke was helping her.

'You know what this girl's been hiding from me?' Luke said at once. His eyes were gleaming.

'Now, Luke,' Olive said. She reddened but didn't look like she really wanted to stop him.

'We're gonna have our own little cow poke,' Luke went on unabashed. 'Why she never shot me for a knucklehead I don't know. No woman ever lived with more real sand in her craw.' That was inelegant, too, maybe, but Olive liked it.

'I agree,' Pick said heartily, 'and congratulations, folks. You had a rough ride, Olive. Do any damage?'

'It worried me a little,' Olive admitted, 'but I seem to be all right. The event's a long ways off.'

She was happy, Pick knew. For the first time she had been a vital part of her community. In the test she had not found herself wanting. It made a tremendous difference. If they survived what might be a more desperate onslaught Olive would take her place in the Hueco.

CHAPTER SEVENTEEN

Hosea with him, Pick rode back to the high meadow in the early dusk. The prisoner was still there, tied to the tree. Gorman had hoped for deliverance by Clover Leaf. He gave evidence of preferring to stay where he was to what he now saw ahead. Pick let him drink at the spring, in no mood to be gentle. This fellow had been all too eager to shoot down helpless men.

'What're you gonna do with me?' Gorman said, wiping the water from his chin.

'I hope to see you hung,' Pick said. They had brought an extra horse, and he ordered the prisoner into the saddle.

Gorman stared down from the leather. 'You don't think Hannegan'll let you turn me in, do you?' he said, trying to be hard about it.

'You've been sweating here all afternoon,' Hosea said. 'Did he show up to help you?'

'He knows damned well I can spill enough—' Gorman said hotly, then he fell silent. Behind his hostility he was growing terrified. He was built to run in a pack and, without one around him, was greatly handicapped.

'Tough man,' Hosea said in a drawl, 'right now they're thinking of nothing but saving their own mangy hides.'

They took the back trail going down to the basin and reached the flat behind Skillet Springs in the early dark. Briefly Pick said, 'Take him on to Luke's, Hosea. I'll poke around a little.'

'What direction?'

'The day I went in to get Packwood I found a place to watch what went on at Clover Leaf. It wouldn't hurt to know when they jump and in what direction.'

'Sure you know what you're doing?'

'Only what I'm not going to do,' Pick said. 'And that's set and wait for them.'

'You're the boss,' Hosea said, but he looked worried.

Pick struck off across the flat toward Mesa, the desert's swift twilight soon deepening into night. He took the notch under Eagle Point and climbed to the bench. He skirted the back side of the blocky uplift and pressed on toward the highly dangerous hills.

Across the lonely distance he could see a light that pinpointed the spot where Piper was waiting out the tense hours. He had seen two contrasting transitions. Olive had developed the steel needed to go with her woman's gentleness of nature. Piper had lost enough of her hardness to become all the more desirable a woman. The desert never failed to modify its dwellers.

He passed the end of the relocated fence line and slipped into the hills. It was easy to retrace the route he had followed coming in before. The night's quiet lay about him, and the inky hills enfolded him. He rode without pause until he came to the knob from which he had descended to make Packwood his prisoner. In the night he could remain seated in the saddle until he got his bearings. For wary moments he waited there, alertly, watching the scene below him.

There was enough star shine to show him the horses in the ranchyard. It had taken time for Hannegan to assemble his scattered crew. Now they were trying to figure out the steps necessary to pull their chestnuts out of the fire. Packwood would be there with them, and he wondered how much hide the rancher had taken off his reckless foreman. The bunkhouse and cookshack blazed with light, but the main house was dark.

It struck him that they were waiting for the deeper night to move again. And however much they sought a less reckless step they could, in the end, find only one solution. That was to wipe out the danger by destroying it utterly. Then there would be no one around to dispute the explanation they gave.

Time was on Pick's side in this. He wondered what chance he had to run off those waiting horses. That would immobilize the big outfit for hours more, long enough for the sheriff to arrive, maybe. The idea appealed to him, and he was ready to take the one-in-a-thousand chance of succeeding with it. He rode quietly into the Clover Leaf meadow. There he began to work his way toward the headquarters compound.

By following a wash he got in fairly close. The sand muffled the sound made by the horse as it moved forward. When he climbed the bank, gun in hand, he saw the big Clover Leaf yard just across. He could even hear the sound of urgently running voices indoors.

He studied the position of the horses, all saddled and standing with dropped reins. They were ready to pound out when riders hit their backs. He could see seven, two immediately in front of the bunkhouse. The others were over toward the big house under the trees. Abruptly he drove in his spurs, ripping out a Comanche yell, and charged forward.

As he came into the yard he aimed directly toward the four animals farthest from the bunkhouse. Trained to stand though they were, the racketing horse and rider broke them into a wheeling, head-slinging run to the south.

Pick twisted in the saddle and saw the bunkhouse door fly open. He drove a shot toward it, and the door slammed shut. He fired again, knocking out the door glass. That was enough to stampede the two horses over there. They bolted. Yelling and cursing issued from the bunkhouse. It prompted Pick to drill yet another shot through the panel of the door.

He lined out, following the horses that went thundering into the south hills. They constituted two thirds of Clover Leaf's ready mount. They pounded ahead of him, reins flying, and he meant to keep them going as long as possible.

For some two miles the escaping horses clung to the main draw through the hills. Then, singly and in pairs, they began to break off. They left the bottom and streaked into some side canyon or patch of brush. That was good enough for Pick's purpose. Recovering them would now be a job needing light to see. He pulled down his horse, a little surprised by his success. Yet he had gained only a small advantage, and it would soon be dissipated.

He waited there long enough to eject the empties from his gun and slip in fresh loads. Excitement swirled in him, focusing in a diamond-hard point. He rode back down the draw, keeping over on the right edge, alert for the sound of pursuit.

The outfit had mustered the courage to pour out of the bunkhouse and discover it was not besieged. From the trees in the wash Pick viewed the running about and heard the unintelligible shouting. He wondered if they knew two horses had headed north. They could have stopped running close enough in to be recovered by a man on foot. He put down the temptation to disorganize them again with more shooting. He rode on, intending to drive those two horses on out of reach.

A couple of minutes later he saw he had crowded his luck too hard. Riders came toward him from the north. They were out in the widening bottom of the bay and due ahead. He realized there were only two mounted horses, behind which two others were being led. Clover Leaf had posted sentries down there to guard against an attack from the basin. He had worked around them unwittingly by slipping in through the hills. The sentries had seen the charging horses, caught them, and were taking them back to see what had gone wrong. Pick knew he had been seen already. He drove toward them in a rushing charge. He saw them drop the led horses. Fire ripped open the night, and guns rapped out. He shot back, for he had to drive past them or be driven back to Clover Leaf.

The bullet caught him somewhere around the hip, nearly knocking him out of the saddle. He grabbed the horn, swaying widely. The shock of hammered bone rolled to his brain, dazing and blinding him. His reckless, continuing drive split the forward pair apart. He triggered a shot at the man on his right, and the man spilled out of the saddle.

He wheeled around to see that the other had broken off and was heading for Clover Leaf at a dead run. The blackness slugged at Pick's brain. He rode warily to where the rider lay unmoving on the ground. It was Shorty

Halleck who would fight no more.

Knowing Clover Leaf riders would be all over the area soon, Pick made for the western hills. The numbness stayed in his hip and side, and he knew he was bleeding badly. He might not last long enough to reach Big Springs. That gave him one chance, to make it to the Tarrone place where the women could help him.

He found he couldn't ride faster than a slow trot and still stay in the saddle. He steeled himself against the urge to risk a greater speed. It was hard to do. The mounted rider would bring a new mount out of Clover Leaf's horse pasture. That would put the whole outfit in the saddle.

Slowed against his will, he changed direction, picking his way along the edge of the hills. Finally he deemed it safe to turn across the open flat toward Gap Springs and save time. His body had begun to thaw, and pain shot along his hip and side. His foot squashed in the blood slowly filling his boot.

This would get worse. He reached Gap Springs with a mounting dread of the three or four miles yet to ride to Piper's place. He decided to turn in and see what he could find in Finney's old shack to take care of himself.

He would never get back on the horse again, so he would make his stand there. He reined the horse over toward the house.

He was too spent and dazed to feel anything

much when a voice fell across the night.

'Stop right there.'

'Piper,' he said in relief. 'It's Pick. What're you doing way up here?'

She came out of the brush at the end of the house and ran toward him. 'You said to watch for the sheriff. So I come up where I'd see him when he come through the gap. You gave me a turn. I thought it was a Clover Leaf man and I was in trouble. Now, what are you doing up here?'

'I got in a little jangle,' Pick said, 'and I need help.'

'You're hurt?'

'Got one in the—leg, I think, but pretty close to the hip. It kind of hobbles me. You'll have to help me get down.'

She was already rushing to him. He all but fell from the saddle; she kept him upright. To his relief he could stand, so the bone wasn't shattered. If they could check the bleeding, he'd get along a while yet. Still it was a slow, hard job moving over into the shack.

'We don't dare have a light,' Pick said. 'Feel around in the closet for some rags. That's all we can do right now.'

A gusty breath came out of him, and the room swayed. He lay back on the bunk that she had helped him reach. He heard her moving, but the impression was that she was a mile off. He heard the sound of ripping cloth.

He heard her say, 'I found a knife. I'm going

211

to cut off your pants leg.'

'Rip and lay it back,' Pick said. 'Where is it?'

'You're bleeding from the pocket down. Anybody after you?'

'Will be—before long. Get me tied up. Then I want you to go to Big Springs and warn them.'

'There's plenty of men over there, and I'm not leaving you alone.' He slipped back into the swirling mists until her far-off voice spoke again. 'There. That ought to check it. You lay there now. I'm going to hide your horse in the barn with mine.'

He tried to tell her again to head for Big Springs, anywhere it was safer, but she had already slipped from the room. That was all he knew until he heard the crack of a rifle right at hand.

A man's voice called from beyond the wall, 'Come out of there, Atherton. You ain't got a chance.' Pick knew the voice. It belonged to Hannegan.

That burned the fog out of his brain. He shoved to a sit, then rocked onto his feet, weaving there while he located Piper. She stood beside the window from which she had knocked the glass. She was staring out into the hostile night. He lurched toward her.

'Let me have the rifle,' he said quietly.

She ignored him. 'There's three of them,' she said. 'One's Hannegan, and I think another's Packwood.'

'They split into bunches to run me down before they go any farther. Where are they?'

'I drove them into the brush. For a minute I thought they'd ride by; then they decided to look at this place.'

By then Pick's pistol was in his hand. He had no intention of letting them riddle the shack with Piper in it. He stepped to the door. He heard her hissed objection but opened the door. He raised his voice to a shout.

'I'm coming out, Hannegan.'

'With your hands up and empty.'

They had heard a rifle. Pick hoped desperately that for a moment they would think that was the only weapon he had. He slipped the six-gun under the band of his pants, lifted his hands, and moved out to the step. He halted there, barely able to stand erect.

'Keep coming,' Hannegan said from the brush.

'I can't. Got one—in the leg.'

'We're all covering you,' Hannegan said. 'Don't try anything. I'm coming in.'

Pick knew that he stood only a faint chance of getting one of them before they dropped him. But it would give Piper her chance at them, her one hope of saving herself. He saw the outline of a figure at the edge of the brush. He stabbed his hand for his gun.

Others cracked open the night out there. He heard Piper's rifle roar just back of him.

He saw fire redden in daubs ahead, and his own gun kept spitting flame and lead. Then something hit him like worlds colliding, and he was out of the fight.

*   *   *

He'd had other fantasies running in his fevered head, but none so vivid or protracted. He seemed captured for all time in a very real unreality in which pain was the prime stuff of life. These things were mostly in the hot core of his brain, although a thumping ache came from somewhere lower on his body. Then all at once he opened his eyes to daylight and the fact that he was in his own room at Mesa.

But not alone. He rolled his head to see Piper looking down at him. The turning made her image swim and his head roar. He closed his eyes, and when he opened them again she was in focus, her background steady.

'You're—all right,' he said.

She smiled. 'You've got a cracked skull, but it looks like you are, too. You sure had us scared a while.'

'What about—Clover Leaf?'

'That outfit's dissolved. Between us we got Packwood and Hannegan at Finney's shack. That cut the head off the snake. Some of the punchers cleared out of the country. Gorman spilled enough, there's no charges against our side.'

'The sheriff?'

'He's come and gone,' Piper said. 'So has the doctor. But you keep quiet. You've been there three days and you need rest.'

'I'll be quiet when I'm done talking,' Pick said. 'How about you and your mother moving over here to Mesa? What I mean is, I—I—'

'I know what you mean,' Piper said. 'Ma wouldn't want to. She'd rather stay there and keep house for Rip.'

'And you?'

Piper said very softly, 'I've already moved in, Pick.'

We hope you have enjoyed this Large Print book. Other Chivers Press or G.K. Hall & Co. Large Print books are available at your library or directly from the publishers.

For more information about current and forthcoming titles, please call or write, without obligation, to:

Chivers Press Limited
Windsor Bridge Road
Bath BA2 3AX
England
Tel. (01225) 335336

OR

G.K. Hall & Co.
P.O. Box 159
Thorndike, Maine 04986
USA
Tel. (800) 223-2336

All our Large Print titles are designed for easy reading, and all our books are made to last.